Too Kölsch For Comfort

Victoria Hamel

PB & A Publishing

Also By Victoria Hamel

Book One in the Marley Creek Romance Series

No Gouda Without You

Get your copy of book two here: https://a.co/d/0avDaHZ

And Coming this Summer:

Book Three in the Marley Creek Romance Series

Is This Love Fur Real?

Preorder your copy here: https://a.co/d/8e7WOW3
Sign up for Victoria's free newsletter to stay up to date on her
book news:
https://deft-crafter-9476.ck.page/profile

Contents

Chapter One

♥

ZAINA

Zaina Evans knew a blister was brewing on her big toe. Lucky for her, it was so cold her feet were going numb in her running shoes. They didn't call this the Frosty Toes 10K for nothing. She passed mile marker four and bemoaned her current state. *Why did I sign up to do this run?* She didn't answer herself because she knew the answer. On New Year's Eve, she'd declared this was going to be her year.

She was moving on, and she wouldn't wallow anymore. Wallowing was so last year. Mike had broken up with her back in October, and she'd let that get to her for too long! She was freezing right now, but at least she wasn't lying in bed, unshowered, eating a bag of chips, scrolling social media, and being mad at people who were happy. The wind picked up from the north, slicing through her knit cap, sweatshirt, and leggings.

She knew this would be the slowest race she'd ever run, but all that mattered was finishing. Zaina would never again let a man stop her from doing the things she wanted to do. Better to be alone and happy! Mike had complained whenever she went for a run. He'd even had the nerve to say that she didn't look cute in her running gear, so during their dating she'd donated her lightweight but warm layers of winter-appropriate running clothes. Fast forward to today, here she was freezing cold and running against a biting wind with three thousand of her fellow Marley Creek residents. She'd caught the meteorologist on TV before she'd left for the race, and she'd said they were having the coldest start to January on record. "Never again," she gasped into the wind.

She probably should have waited until April to run a race, but she wanted to start the year by getting off her couch, so here she was. Frosty toes, frosty nose, frosty everything. She shook out her arms and tried to pick up her pace. Back in the day, she'd been able to run eight-minute miles, but today she was slower than molasses.

She turned a corner and saw her best friend, Devin Belmont, the mayor of Marley Creek, jumping up and down. "Go Zaina! Ben's already finished and gotten us a table at Hop's Heaven!"

Zaina wanted to cry, but if she did, the tears would just freeze to her face. Her lips felt numb. She licked them and shouted back to Devin, "Why did I do this to myself?"

Devin shrugged. "You said this was going to be your year!"

Zaina grimaced and kept plodding along. Soon, she could almost make out the finish line banner ahead of her. It looked like it was still half a mile away. Other runners were few and far between now. Either Zaina was one of the last stragglers trying to finish or everyone else had been smart enough to give up, especially now that the wind was blowing snow onto the road, hiding patches of ice. Zaina should have spent the last few weeks training more often for this run and spending less time on her couch eating ice cream and streaming Korean Dramas.

She took in a deep breath through her nose and out of her mouth. "One, two, three, four," she counted to regulate her breathing.

In K-Dramas, life was simple. If it was a workplace drama, the universe and quirky coworkers conspired to get the main couple stuck together on work projects or locked in a storage closet. In a fantasy, the main couple would overcome any obstacles thrown at them because they were fated to be together. At some point, they would recognize their love interest was their one-true-love reincarnated. The music would swell at all the right points in the plot and there was always a happy ending. Why couldn't she find her true love? Maybe that wasn't her path. She told herself it was time to see if she could be alone and happy. Zaina even imagined what it would be like to be a single parent. Being a mom didn't mean she had to have a husband.

If her best friend Nicole was running next to her, Nicole would remind Zaina that soulmates were a terrible idea. Nicole would say, "Why should we be trapped for eternity only knowing one love?" Zaina admitted there were flaws, but part of her still craved the romantic ideal of finding your better half, the one and only love to last all your years, however impractical and unlikely.

As she made her way against the wind, Zaina thought about how many years she'd been dating and hoping each man she dated was the one, only to wind up alone, again and again. She was done wasting her time looking for love. She was running faster now and the heat of her anger was making the cold wind feel like a welcome summer breeze. The finish line was coming into focus, and a sign posted on the side of the road announced she was hitting the six-mile mark. *Only a little further!* She began pumping her arms harder.

Pride swelled in her chest. She put one foot in front of the other, looking straight ahead as she focused on the finish line. There were more spectators now that she was so close to the end. She let their clapping and shouting cheer her on. She glanced over at the sidelines and saw a man wearing a giant beer mug costume. *What the?* She thought and realized it was Jasper Kane. *Ugh.* She'd almost forgotten he was the main sponsor of the Frosty Toes 10k. Zaina picked up her speed now. She would not let Jasper distract her. Just seeing his smug face ticked her off. She was sure he thought she looked ridiculous; he'd been laughing at her ever since that night sophomore year.

With determination, she stared down the finish line. Nothing could stop her now! Her foot hit a snow-covered spot on the street and she slid. Then her arms were pinwheeling as she tried desperately to stop herself from falling, but she'd been going too fast to quell her momentum. Her knee, right hand, and finally her cheek kissed the ground, hard. She could hear a gasp from the crowd as she tried to pick herself up. *What's the point?* Her knee throbbed. She looked down at her hand, which was a scraped up bloody mess.

A couple of women wearing finisher medals walked toward her. "Are you okay!?" the one with a ponytail shouted.

Her vision blurred from tears of humiliation more than pain. The adrenaline was staving off the pain from her bleeding, and surely bruised body, for now. Behind the women, a large yellow and brown blob was rushing toward her. The blob passed them and it took a moment for it to click. The blob was Jasper. *Great, he probably wants to come gloat. Zaina made a fool of herself. Nothing has changed since high school.*

The sharp contours of his face stood out around the massive white fuzzy wig he wore. *That must be the suds,* she thought. Jasper squatted down in front of her. His deep brown eyes stared into hers and the concern she saw in them startled her. He seemed to be worried about her? Then again, he was the sponsor for this event. Maybe he was worried about getting sued. She'd signed a waiver, but she probably could still sue, if she was that type of person.

"Zaina," Jasper said, searching her face, "are you okay?"

Zaina nodded.

"Let's get you to the finish line."

Her mouth dropped open. "I can't."

Jasper frowned. "Is it your knee? You can't walk?"

"I don't know. I'm afraid to get up."

The two women hung back a few feet. "Do you need help? Should we call an ambulance?" One asked.

Zaina's face reddened. "Oh, gosh no! Please don't!"

Jasper leaned in and spoke so only Zaina could hear. "If you want to finish this thing, let me help you."

Zaina touched her cheek; it was burning now. She looked down at her hand, happy to see it had stopped bleeding. "I feel so stupid. Maybe I should just wait here for the street to swallow me up." She bit her bottom lip. Why was she telling Jasper Kane of all people how she felt? She must have a concussion.

Jasper chuckled, his dark eyes lighting up. "It's a little early for pothole season. C'mon, you've got this."

He held out his gloved hand, and she took it. *Wait until I tell Nicole and Devin about this. They won't believe it.* He slowly helped her up, and then she was standing.

"Can you walk?" asked the other lady who'd been standing with her friend.

Jasper kept hold of Zaina's uninjured hand and wrapped his other arm around her waist. "Are you okay with my arm here?"

Zaina nodded to Jasper and spoke to the woman, "Let's see." She took a tentative step. Her ankle was fine, but her knee really hurt. She took another step, and her knee felt a little better. "There is no way I can keep running." Her heart dropped. She needed a win.

"Who says you need to keep running to finish this race? Let's do it together."

The hate she'd kept in her heart for Jasper since high school shrunk a bit. Later, she could ask herself what was in it for him, but for now, she'd let him help her finish.

"Fine, it's only what? Half a block?" she panted.

"Sure, let's go with that, half a block." He gave her a gentle squeeze and took a bigger step.

Jasper had almost a foot of height on her, and she took three steps to his one.

If she was going to finish this race, she needed to lean on him, literally. Zaina relaxed into Jasper's grip and began a shuffle walk-run. Her knee ached, but at least it wasn't locking up or getting worse with movement. She knew the ache in her knee wasn't nearly equal to the hit her pride would take if she didn't finish this damn race.

Behind her, she could hear the two ladies who'd come to her rescue chatting. "Isn't he just the cutest? Even in that silly costume."

Zaina was glad the silly costume meant Jasper had very limited peripheral vision and couldn't see her beet-red face. She tried to pick up the pace, desperate to get to the finish line.

"You're doing great Zaina; we're almost there. Everyone is cheering you on!" He bobbed his head in her direction and the suds rubbed her face.

"Ouch," she gasped, but kept moving.

"D-did I knock into you?" He turned toward her. She was surprised to see his brows were lowered in concern.

"It's okay."

"Sorry about that. This costume seemed like a great idea when I ordered it."

"No worries," Zaina said. "It's fine."

The crowd that had been milling around the finish line now stood watching Zaina and Jasper's slow movement to the finish line. There was cheering, and some spectators were blasting air horns. The race Master of Ceremonies, who was also the newest barback at Hop's Heaven, started playing "Eye of the Tiger" by Survivor on the sound system.

"Zaina's up," Jasper began singing off key.

Zaina chuckled, and Jasper seemed to take that as a sign to sing louder.

"Back on her feeeeet!"

Zaina's chuckle turned into guffaws as they continued walk-running. Jasper's arm was holding her tight, but not restrictive.

"Hurt my hand, hurt my knee-eee." Zaina began singing along with Jasper as she hobbled along the last few meters of the race.

"And she's not gonna fall something something of the tiger!!!!" They sang together as she, well, they crossed the finish line. "And the crowd goes wild," Jasper whispered in her ear as he released her.

"Thank you for helping me finish the race. It was important for me to do this," she explained.

"That's what I'm here for," Jasper said, and Zaina looked at him confused.

She opened her mouth to speak when the guy working the sound system announced,
"Jasper Kane, Jasper Kane, you're needed in the big tent for the awards ceremony."

Jasper put his hand on the shoulder Zaina hadn't fallen on. "Don't forget to get your complimentary beer, and ice that knee!" He took off in a jog toward the brewery.

She shrugged. "Oh, well," she said out loud and began limping toward the refreshment line.

"Zaina! Over here!"

Zaina looked over and waved. Devin and her husband, Ben, were walking over to her. Devin was wearing boots with jeans and a long puffy jacket. She had a knit cap over her braids and a long-crocheted scarf of gold and maroon around her neck. Zaina knew Devin thought maroon and gold didn't look good on her, but it was the school colors for Marley Creek High School, and this was a reelection year. Ben stood holding his wife's hand. He was wearing his finisher's medal and a Marley

Creek High knit hat. Clearly, Devin had made sure he'd put that on.

Devin handed Ben her beer and gave Zaina a big hug. "You did it! I knew you could!"

"Thanks, but did you see me wipe out?"

Devin brushed off Zaina's shoulders, "I did, oof, how are you feeling?"

"I'm not going to go viral, am I?"

Devin shook her head, "No, by the time you fell, almost everyone was done running and either heading over or already in line for the free beer. I'm sure everyone was too busy getting their beer and donut to notice your fall."

Zaina blew out a sigh of relief, "Thank the goddess for that."

Ben chimed in, "But, when Jasper helped you up and you two started making your way to the finish—"

"—and then the Eye of the Tiger started playing," Devin interrupted.

Ben nodded. "That got people's attention. When you crossed the finish line—"

"It was sweet! A real feel-good kind of moment." Devin chose her words carefully, "if it goes viral, and it probably won't, I don't think you'll be made into a gif."

"That's good, I guess?" Her knee, hand, and face were really smarting now. She looked at her friend Devin and lightly touched where her cheek had hit the ground.

"How does it look? Do you think I'm going to have a black eye?"

Devin frowned and took her beer back from her husband. "Ben, run and go get a couple of icepacks for Zaina. Quick, before the medical tent is taken down."

Ben gave his wife a quick kiss on her forehead and took off at a jog.

Devin wrapped her arm around Zaina's and turned toward the post-race recovery area. "Now let's go get you your medal."

Chapter Two

♥

JASPER

Jasper bustled around the taproom, connecting with everyone who'd come out for the race, be it long time runners who finished the race in record time or moms with strollers who'd been on the sidelines. His chest filled with pride as he soaked in the standing room only area inside and the crowd outside under repurposed Oktoberfest tent. It was a good thing he'd gotten the tent put up for today, given the below normal temps. Of course, it didn't take a rocket scientist to expect near zero temperatures in January.

Jasper continued to shake hands and compliment anyone wearing a medal on finishing the Frosty Toes 10k. He invited them to come back to the brewery for trivia night and let them know about the upcoming Friday night bands. He was still clad in his beer mug costume and sweat was trickling down Jasper's back. He walked around the bar and back to his office. Once inside, he took off the big fluffy white wig of beer foam and blew out a sigh of relief as his temperature quickly regulated. He ran a hand through his shoulder length dark brown hair.

"Mr. Kane, you gotta check this out!"

Jasper looked up to see his current charity case employee waving a phone. "What's up, Ethan?"

Ethan walked into the office and held out his phone to Jasper. "You're freaking trending!" He clicked a video and Jasper saw himself and Zaina crossing the finish line, singing along with the music blasting in the background and the crowd cheering.

The caption said, "Find you a man that will get you across the finish line. #goals #eyeofthetiger #HEA #runningstrong."

"No kidding." Jasper smiled slowly. He loved free publicity.

"You've already got thousands of shares."

Jasper's smile now went up to his dark brown eyes. "Already?"

Ethan nodded vigorously.

Jasper held out his hand. "Let me see your phone again." Jasper towered over Ethan who was maybe five feet, six inches. While Jasper was over six feet tall and lean, Ethan had the shape of a serious bodybuilder. His short, cropped bleached blonde hair was also the opposite of Jasper's raven waves. Jasper pushed back his hair and replayed the video.

"Will you look at that? They tagged us in the video." Jasper slapped Ethan on the back. "Looks like we're going viral! Do me a favor; I need my phone. Help me unzip this costume."

Jasper turned around. Ethan had to stand on his tiptoes to grab the zipper. "Well, this is awkward." Ethan said.

"You're telling me."

Jasper sighed in relief as the zipper came down to the middle of his back. However, now he could also feel Ethan's hot breath against his neck. He moved to the side. "Okay, I'm good. Thanks for the help."

Jasper pulled off the front of his costume and slid his phone out of his pocket. He unlocked it, and a flood of notifications filled his screen. Curious, he opened the Hop's Heaven account and saw that it had gotten over twenty thousand new likes in the last hour. He checked his DMs and saw one from a local morning television show. They wanted to know if he'd be interested in a remote on Friday morning.

Jasper's jaw dropped. This was fantastic. They would come out to Hop's Heaven and do their show live from the brewery. This was exactly the break he needed. He'd built up Hop's Heaven from nothing and now he was ready to expand. He just needed to find investors to buy into his concept. His goal had always been to go national before he was forty and this was just the exposure to do it.

He took a hair tie and pulled his hair off his neck, twisting it into a topknot. He leaned back on his desk and responded to the producer.

Ethan hovered next to him. "Hop's Heaven is trending on YouTube and TikTok."

"This is just the beginning," Jasper said as his thumbs moved at the speed of light.

"I can't say I've ever been part of anything going viral before."

Jasper looked at Ethan. Ethan had washed out of college and had been living with his dad until his stepmom had given his father an ultimatum. Ethan's dad has asked Sean, his oldest son and Jasper's best friend, to take in his stepbrother. Sean owned Jesse's Pub, and he'd tried to put Ethan to work in the kitchen as a line chef trainee. That had been a disaster. Then he'd tried bussing tables, and you'd think with his muscles he'd have done well, but according to Sean, Ethan was unfailingly too quick to clear the tables, upsetting guests and servers alike.

Sean had begged Jasper to take pity on him and take Ethan off his hands. Jasper had agreed a few weeks ago. If Jasper had to sum up his experience with Ethan so far, he would say it had been tolerable. Of course, all he'd had Ethan do so far was clean up. Clean up the bathrooms, clean up the tap room. Shovel snow, and salt outside. Perhaps Ethan could help with social media. He was a good-looking guy. Maybe he could help bring in more of the early 20s crowd. Then again, did Jasper want his brewery filled with twenty-two-year-old kids? He shook his head. Maybe, maybe not.

His phone chimed. A reply from the producer already! They only had one request. Could Jasper make sure the runner whom he'd helped cross the finish line was at the brewery on Friday to be part of the morning show? They'd like to interview them together on Friday as part of their weekly Feel Good Friday show.

Jasper chewed on his bottom lip. He should have known they'd ask for Zaina to be part of the show. If she wasn't part of the show, it wouldn't be very much of a feel good Friday, would it?

This is your chance. You've been working for years to get a break like this. Just say yes, she'll be there and then figure out how to talk Zaina into it. Jasper blew out a deep breath and felt the adrenaline flooding into his arms and legs. He answered, confirming that Zaina Evans would be delighted to be featured on Channel Twelve's Feel Good Friday. He doubled checked his spelling, added an exclamation point and sent the reply. *Now I just need to make sure she'll show up. If only I had some leverage over her.*

"Ethan, looks like we are going to stay viral for a while."

"How so?"

"Channel Twelve is going to do their Friday morning show here this week."

Ethan's eyes widened. "Feel Good Friday is happening here?"

Jasper cocked his head and squinted, "You know about Feel Good Friday? I've never heard of it until today, and I grew up in Marley Creek."

"I watch the Channel Twelve morning show every day when I go to the gym. I never miss a Feel Good Friday. It's always so inspiring. A few weeks ago, they were at a retirement village that has opened a day care facility. It's called Raising Them Forward. Residents take classes and then they work in the daycare. It's been a tremendous success; the retired people love spending time with the little kids and the kids basically have all these bonus grandparents."

Jasper noticed this was the most animated he'd ever seen Ethan. "Yes, that sounds like a nice program."

Ethan smiled, "And this past week they said the daycare facility got a special grant from AARP to expand the program, all because of Channel Twelve's Feel Good Friday!"

Jasper slapped his hand on his desk. "Now that's what I'm talking about! Think about what that kind of publicity could do for Hop's Heaven!"

"Yes, maybe then we could have Mugs for Pugs Night."

"Mugs for Pugs night?"

"Yes, pug dogs often have breathing problems."

"Because their faces are mushed?" Jasper asked off-hand.

Ethan nodded vigorously, "Exactly. So, Mugs for Pugs is a nonprofit that raises money to fund surgeries for pugs who can't afford it otherwise."

"You mean the owners can't afford the surgery?"

Ethan shrugged. "Same difference."

"So, how does it work?"

"You give a dollar for every drink to Mugs for Pugs, and they give surgery grants."

"How'd you hear about this?"

"I volunteer at the Marley Creek Animal Shelter on Mondays."

"You've only been here for a couple of months." Jasper was surprised, Ethan had more layers than college-dropout gym rat implied.

Ethan shrugged. "I started volunteering at an animal shelter when I was in high school. Is there anything better than playing with kittens or puppies when life has you down?"

"Well," Jasper said, waggling his eyebrows.

Ethan shook his head.

"How can I capitalize on this?" Jasper pondered.

"Mugs for Pugs, like I said."

"Right, I got that, but there needs to be something more, something to get people invested and following Hop's Heaven to the point they wish there was a Hop's Heaven in their neighborhood."

Ethan shrugged. "I don't think I can help you there."

"That's why I'm the owner and CEO, and you're..."

Ethan frowned. "I should get back to work."

"Yes, you should." Having dismissed Ethan, Jasper went back to looking at his phone. He rocked on his heels, full of energy, envisioning the possibilities this viral moment was going to give him. He could see it now, Hop's Heavens in Boston, MA, Charlotte, NC, Denver, Co, Phoenix, AZ. He visualized himself cutting the ribbon on his second location. Should he wear a suit for the occasion or stick with his usual casual jeans, flannel and a logo T-shirt? Maybe he should look into a bespoke suit. It was even possible, if he started wearing a suit, at least at professional meetings, his mother would stop crapping all over his business.

He made a note to research buying a custom suit and went back to see what the Internet had to say about the video. It was still trending. *Fantastic*, he thought. As he scrolled through the comments, he noticed one clear theme. The comments were filled with hearts and people saying the hot guy in the beer mug costume and the tiny runner girl would make a great couple. Jasper paced his office. He knew Zaina didn't care for him. She'd made that clear many times over the years. At this point, whenever Zaina looked at him, he felt like he had 'asshole' tattooed on his forehead.

Their past was going to make things harder, but nothing he couldn't talk his way through. All he needed to do was find a way to talk Zaina into giving the people what they wanted—as an act of course, then he could translate their short viral moment into investors and franchisees. Last year, He'd looked into being on a couple of reality TV shows to raise his visibility on social media, but that involved time away from his business and a loss of control over the content the TV shows would want to generate so he hadn't moved ahead.

Zaina falling was a godsend! Now he could get that same attention on his terms, and if he could talk Zaina into a fake relationship for their mutual benefit, would that be any different from doing a reality show? It was all an illusion. A marketing scheme, and he was good at marketing.

He left his office and walked back out to the bustling tasting room. Thanks to his height, he could easily scan the room looking for the tiny woman with the pixie haircut and giant icepack on her knee. She was sitting with the mayor of Marley Creek and her husband. As he walked toward the group, she threw her head back and laughed, hitting the table with her hand. He froze for a moment and felt a pang in his chest, remembering a time when a much younger Zaina had laughed like that with him.

Chapter Three

♥

ZAINA

Zaina was sitting at a table in the Hop's Heaven taproom with her best friend, Devin, and Devin's husband, Ben.

Zaina laughed and shook her head. "There is never a dull moment at your house, that's for sure."

Ben clinked his glass against Zaina's. "Truer words have never been spoken."

Devin elbowed her husband playfully. "Those are our precious babies you're talking about."

Ben wrapped his arm around his wife. His brown eyes twinkled behind his glasses. "They get their mischievous side from you, my dear. I was a perfect angel as a child."

"Ha!" Devin laughed. "Your mother would beg to differ. She said by the time you were five she'd gone gray from chasing you around, and she was only 29 at the time!"

Ben smiled a big toothy grin, "let's just split the difference and say that we are high-energy, curious people and those traits have been passed down to our delightful children."

Devin patted her husband's leg. "I can agree with that."

Zaina adjusted her ice pack and sighed. "I can't believe it's been ten years since your wedding. You two are still so in love. Here I am, over thirty-five, which is eighty in dating app years, and I have no prospects."

Devin cocked her head, "What about…"

"Nope," Zaina interrupts, "Turned out he was anti-soap."

Ben leaned forward. "I'm sorry I don't think I heard you correctly. It's pretty loud in here. Did you say anti-soap?"

"Oh, my word," Devin said, shivering, her dark curls bouncing.

"Yep. That man said he saw online soap was bad for your skin, so when he showered, he just let the water rain down on him and then he toweled off."

Ben lifted his glasses up and massaged the bridge of his nose. "He told you this on a date?"

"We were sitting at Miller's Pub downtown and yes, that's when he told me."

"I've got to ask," Devin propped her elbow on the table and put her chin in her palm, "did he smell?"

Zaina's cheeks flushed. "I'm not proud of it, but once he said that, I told him I had to go to the restroom, and I called Nicole. I went back to the table and five minutes later she called me with our standard emergency, and I bailed. I just couldn't do it!"

Ben crossed his arms. "I don't know how you single people do it. The apps and the goofy stuff people believe after they go down a rabbit hole on YouTube or TikTok. It's wild!"

"We are blessed. We were able to avoid all of that," Devin agreed, giving Ben a side hug.

Zaina slumped down, dramatically pouting, "This is exactly what I'm talking about! Why can't I meet a decent man?"

Zaina saw a shadow fall over her, and someone cleared their throat.

"Hey Jasper! Outstanding event today!" Ben stood up and put out his hand to Jasper, who was now standing next to Zaina's chair.

Zaina rolled her eyes and Devin mouthed, "Behave." Zaina took a drink of her beer.

"Pull up a seat, and join us," Ben said, gesturing to the chair Zaina had been using to prop up her leg.

"Alright, I've got a few minutes."

He looked down at the chair and then at Zaina. "How are you doing?" He asked with a crooked smile.

"Fine," she said flatly.

Devin cleared her throat.

"I mean, I am doing okay. Thanks for your help." Zaina slightly smiled.

"You're welcome. I couldn't leave a man down on the battlefield."

Zaina snickered. "That sleet was definitely pelting me out there. You sure picked a terrible day for the race."

Jasper held up his hands. "Don't blame it all on me. The mayor," he held up one hand and used his other hand to point toward Devin, "and the town council had the final decision on the day."

Zaina leaned over and spoke to her friend, "Ah, so this is all your fault."

"It wouldn't be a Frosty 10K if we had it in March." Devin held out her hand, palm up.

Everyone took a sip of their beers, except Jasper, who didn't have one, and silence fell at the table.

"Well, all's well that ends well, I guess!" Ben exclaimed.

"Yes, thank you, Jasper, for helping Zaina finish the race," Devin said.

"Like I said, I was happy to help Zaina finish."

Zaina adjusted her ice pack again and hoped Jasper would leave the table so she could get back to relaxing with her friends. "Yes, thank you very much Jasper, I appreciate the assist, and I'm sure you have lots of work to do, and we'll let you get back to your brewery."

Jasper leaned over to make eye contact with Zaina. "Actually, I was wondering if I could talk to you for a moment?"

Ben and Devin exchanged a look, and then they looked at Zaina.

Zaina scowled. She should have expected this. Jasper probably wanted her to thank him some more. The man was the worst. She should have told him to go away when he offered to help her. This would teach her not to take the hand being held out to her.

Ben looked at his watch. "You know what? It's already noon, and we told the babysitter we'd be home by now, didn't we?"

Devin nodded her head slowly, "Yes, yes! That's right, we need to get going! Can't leave the babysitter waiting for us!"

"But you haven't finished your drinks!" Zaina said.

"Sorry Z, babysitters talk to each other. We can't lose another one. I'll text you later."

Ben was already up and had his coat on. He clapped Jasper on the back, "Great to see you, Jasper." Ben held up Devin's coat so she could put it on.

Zaina continued, trying to make eye contact, "I could give you a ride home, Devin, if you wanted to stay?"

"Oh hon, I wish I could…"

She leaned over and gave Zaina a brief hug. "Be good," she admonished quietly in Zaina's ear.

"Take me with you," Zaina whispered back.

Devin gave her a big hug and then took Ben's hand and off they went, leaving Jasper and Zaina alone at the table.

"What did you need to talk to me about?" Zaina asked.

"Have you been on your phone since the race ended?"

"No, why?" Zaina scrunched up her face.

Jasper pulled out his phone, unlocked it, and scrolled to TikTok. "Check this out." He scooted his chair closer to her and leaned over so she could see the screen clearly. Zaina held herself ramrod straight. He had a warmth radiating off him and she could smell him, the citrus of hops plus a scent that reminded her of one incense she stocked at her shop, New Age Stones and Witch Crafts. The incense was called Tranquil Nights, and it was one of her go-to's when she was feeling stressed. *Oh, the irony. He smells like calm, but he only stresses me out.*

She bit her lip to stop herself from laughing and continued looking down at Jasper's screen.

"Ready to see this?"

"Yeah, whatever."

"Just wait." Jasper smiled widely and hit play.

Zaina's eyes widened. She watched the flood of comments scroll the screen behind which she and Jasper were singing and shuffle-running across the finish line. She was stunned to see the giant grin on her face, but nothing could have prepared her for the look on Jasper's face. His eyes were locked on her face, and they were filled with kindness and something more? Her lips twisted; he was looking as if she was a treasure. *What was going on, Zaina, get a grip. You know he doesn't care about anyone but himself.* Hearts and comments saying Zaina and Jasper were adorable and wondering if they were dating scrolled up the screen as the video finished playing.

Jasper pulled back his phone and stopped the video that was beginning to replay. He fiddled with his phone for a moment before looking up.

Zaina heaved a sigh and said, "Well?"

Jasper tapped his fingers on the table, "What do you think?"

Zaina just looked at him. "About what?"

"We're viral! Can you believe it? This video has over half a million views."

"For real? Wow, that's more than any post I've ever made by far, but so what?"

Jasper leaned in, "Don't you see? This is my chance. Well, let me rephrase. This major free publicity has fallen into our laps, and I'm going to make sure we squeeze everything out of this. I'm going places and you can go places too."

"Simmer down Tony Robbins, maybe translate whatever you are talking about into English instead of business productivity jargon," Zaina moved to cross her legs and winced as her leg brushed her sore knee.

Jasper paused and searched her face. "Are you okay? Let me get a chair for you to prop your foot." Jasper put down his phone, pushed back his chair, and walked around the table. He picked up the chair Devin had been sitting in and brought it over and put it in front of Zaina. "Here, let me help you."

Zaina bent forward and put her hand on her calf. Jasper leaned over and helped her lift her foot onto the chair.

"Do you need another ice pack? The physical therapy docs have left, but I can take some ice and wrap it in a couple of plastic bags for you."

Zaina was shocked by Jasper's concern. This was strange. They usually treated each other with such disdain. And having to see each other had been happening too frequently since Jasper's best friend, Sean, and Zaina's oldest friend in the world, Nicole, had fallen for each other this fall. It was just a matter of time before those two were engaged. *Shoot,* Zaina thought, *I'm going to have to walk down the aisle with Jasper, aren't I?*

Jasper waved his hand in front of Zaina's face. "Hello,"

Zaina started from her depressing daydream about Nicole's wedding. "Sorry, I'm fine. Now what were you saying about the video? What does it matter if we are viral?"

"It's our ticket to making money. I don't have time to go point by point through my business plan, so work with me here."

"Oh geez," Zaina rolled her eyes, "I'm just a girl. I don't understand marketing."

Jasper pushed out a big breath. "Fine." He held up his hands. "This is more about what's in it for me."

"Then what do you even need me for?"

"Here's the thing. You saw all those comments. People want something to root for and they want to root for us."

Zaina felt her chest getting tight. "What are you talking about?"

"Date me, Zaina!" Jasper exclaimed.

"Have you lost your mind?"

"Please, I've never been more clear-eyed. We," Jasper made air quotes, "post some social media content and I use my elevated social media profile to make Hop's Heaven trend, and that interest in the brand helps catapult me into some national recognition. Do you know what national recognition would mean for me?"

"You'd have an even bigger ego than you do now." She batted her eyes and waited for him to continue his rant.

"Ha-ha. You are hysterical as always, Zaina."

Zaina made a keep going gesture with her hand, "Please continue with your evil villain rant."

Jasper shook his head, "Whatever, Zaina, financial success is more important to me than it is to you, obviously."

"Obviously."

"It would help me find investors interested in my franchise."

"Ah," Zaina said, understanding. "You want to franchise this place."

"Exactly, and I'm not above putting on a show to help move that along."

Zaina swallowed exaggeratedly, "I think I just threw up a little in my mouth."

Jasper lowered his brow, "Please, look at me, I'm in my prime. I've got all my hair, great teeth."

Zaina sighed, "I don't like any of this."

Jasper leaned back in his chair and looked toward the ceiling.

Zaina stole a glance at his lean form as he ruminated. His T-shirt was pulled up a little and she could see a few inches of abs. He was fit, that was for sure. She licked her lips.

"Did I tell you about Friday?" Jasper asked.

"No, what's Friday?"

"Have you ever heard of Channel Twelve's Feel Good Friday?"

"Of course, they've been doing that for ages. Who hasn't heard of it?"

"It doesn't matter if anyone hasn't heard of it. The point is Feel Good Friday will be here." He tapped his finger on the table. "This week, and I need you to be a part of it."

"You want to fake date me?"

Jasper grinning from ear to ear, nodded his head and replied, "Now you get it! Yes, think of it like a reality show. This wouldn't be any different. We just do the show on Friday, talk about how I rescued you and how we finished the race together and now we are dating. Then after that, we'll get together a few times and make some content. We can post it on all the Hop's Heaven's socials. And whatever socials you have for your shop." He paused and looked at her. "You do have online shopping?"

"Of course I do. Do you think I'm an idiot?"

"Look, I don't know. Maybe you don't do the Internet because it's bad for your chi or something."

Zaina rolled her eyes and decided not to explain her store to Jasper.

"What do you think? What do you have to lose?"

"Jasper, I don't think this is for me. I appreciate you helping me out today, and I think it's kind of cool that we had a little viral moment, but I'm just not up for all the drama you are talking about."

"I'll handle everything. All you have to do is show up and you can approve all posts and videos before they go live." Jasper offered quickly.

Zaina shook her head, "No, sorry, I don't think this is a good idea." She pulled on her coat.

Jasper stood up. "Are you going to be okay to drive?"

Zaina stood up, leaning on the chair. "Yes, thank the goddess. I'm feeling better." She let go of the chair and stood on her own. "See, I'll be fine."

"Let me at least walk you to your car."

"Are you offering because you are concerned about me or are you planning to talk me into your hairbrained scheme?"

Jasper put his arms back into his beer mug costume and shrugged. "Can't it be a little of both?"

Zaina shook her head and put on her knit cap. "Let's go. I want to get home and soak in the tub."

Jasper had the sense not to make an innuendo.

Zaina clutched Jasper's arm, and they made their way out to the parking lot. The wind had stopped howling, and it had warmed up from earlier. When they arrived at her car, Jasper opened her door for her and made one last plea.

"What if I pay you?"

"To date you?"

"Don't think of it like that. You'd be more of a marketing consultant. I'm not paying you to date me. I'd be paying you for helping me elevate my media presence."

"I don't think so Jasper."

"Just think about it, sleep on it. Is there anything you've been wanting to do or get? Do this with me and you'll have that extra money."

Zaina carefully got in her car, bending her sore leg, and starting her hybrid. Jasper reached out a hand. "Give me your phone."

"What for?"

"I'll put my number in there. Text me when you get home, so I know you made it okay."

Zaina felt a strange flutter in her stomach. *What was that about?* A snide comment died on her tongue. She was too tired for more weird bantering with Jasper. Everything seemed out of character for him since she'd fallen this morning.

She unlocked her phone and pulled up her contacts. Zaina handed the phone to Jasper, who typed in his number.

"Text me when you get home and think about what I said. It'd just be for a few weeks, and I'll pay for your time and your help."

Zaina started her car. "Fine, okay, I'll text you. I really don't think I'm on board for a pretend relationship, but I'll think about it."

"That's all I ask." He shut her door, and she backed out of her space and exited the parking lot.

Chapter Four

♥

JASPER

His mind could not stop buzzing with ideas to turn his viral moment into something big. All he had to do was get Zaina. He was good at reading people, and he was very good at reading Zaina. He knew she couldn't stand him, but today, thanks to the crappy weather, she'd finally looked at him a little differently. And when he'd asked her if there was something she'd like to do if she had extra money, he'd seen the way she'd sat up a little straighter and made eye contact with him. There was something she wanted and all he had to do was let her talk herself into working with him.

Jasper sat in his office. The brewery had been closed for a few hours. He was watching old Feel Good Fridays on YouTube to get a feel for how Friday might go when Channel Twelve came out. He made a note to see if Sean could cater the event and he'd also check with Donnie at Books and Bread to see if they wanted to provide bagels and pastries.

"It's happening," he whispered to himself. He'd been working on building his brewery empire for years now, and he'd felt stagnant the last few years, so going viral could not have happened at a better time. What a break for Zaina to have fallen. He wondered if he would have run to help someone else or if it was because it was Zaina that he'd run to her aid and had the Internet hoping they would date.

If those people knew how he'd treated Zaina back in high school, well, they'd probably want his head on a stake. But that was then, and thank God they didn't have social media at the time. It was bad enough seeing her in the halls, at least they could get away from each other outside of school.

He shook his head. That was almost twenty years ago. She seems to be over it, mostly. He should stay over it too.

Jasper refocused on his computer and noticed it was after ten. He'd been at work since five-thirty a.m. to make sure everything was set up for the race, and with all the excitement over the video, he'd been wired. The adrenaline was finally wearing off, so he powered down his computer, closed his office door and went into the taproom to make sure everything was secure before locking up.

He walked through the darkened space, straightening a few chairs as he went, admiring the soft glow of lights behind the bar. The twelve taps gleamed. He smiled, remembering he'd thought ahead and stocked up on logo merchandise before the Frosty 10K, and hopefully the remaining stock would fly off the shelves on Friday when Channel Twelve came out.

As he locked the front door, he wrestled with calling his mom to tell her about Feel Good Friday. Even though he was well into his thirties and had been running a craft brewery for years now, his mother still didn't think it was a proper business. Now if he'd opened a winery, that would be different. He kicked rocks in the parking lot and shivered in his jacket. The wind had returned with a vengeance. Jasper hoped there wasn't a storm brewing. January was tough enough on his business because of New Year's Resolutions and Dry January. He didn't need more cold and snow.

Speaking of business, he had to figure out how to get Zaina to go along with his plan. She must be struggling with this terrible weather as well. Frankly, he didn't get why anyone would visit her shop on a nice day. He couldn't imagine she was getting much foot traffic when the wind chills were below zero.

Jasper sat in his car and waited for it to warm up. He really should have started the car before he'd left the warm comfort of the brewery. Sometimes he wished he could just live there. It was the only place he felt completely comfortable. Growing up in the biggest house in Marley Creek with parents who prized wealth over all else had meant growing up in a museum instead of a home.

He looked at the text from Zaina again. She had sent him a picture of her leg propped up on a pillow. Folded just above her knee, he could see she was wearing pajama bottoms that were pink and had little black cats on them. His usual instinct when an attractive woman sent him a picture of herself was to flirt his ass off in hopes it would turn into sexting, but this was Zaina, and he was the last person she'd want to sext. He'd sent her a thumbs up emoji.

Because he was a glutton for punishment, he opened his phone and tapped his mother's contact. The phone rang, echoing around his car as he pulled out of the parking lot and headed toward his house.

"Hello there, Jasper," his mother said flatly.

"Hi, Mother, I didn't wake you, did I?"

"No, I was watching the news. They said people aren't going out as much as they used to, so restaurants and bars are suffering. When are you going to give up that bar of yours and find a serious job?"

"Mom, Hop's Heaven's revenues are up this year. Today we hosted the Frosty Toes 10K, over three-thousand people ran the race, and we must have had at least that many spectators."

"Yes, I saw Main Street was closed when I was on my way to church this morning."

"Actually, an interesting thing happened at the run today. There was a runner who fell, and it was someone I went to high school with—Zaina Evans, and I helped her up and we ran across the finish line together."

"Zaina, oh yes, I remember her. You thought you were going to go on a date with her. Thank goodness I nipped that in the bud. What is she up to? Working at a gas station? Or married to a plumber?"

Jasper ground his teeth. "She owns a store in town, New Age Stones and Witch Crafts."

"Even worse, she's a witch! That store probably makes a few hundred bucks profit a year, if that!"

"Mom, I'm sure she makes a decent living, and she's lucky she can do something she loves."

"Pfft, I'm so glad you didn't get mixed up with her. She's going nowhere."

Jasper's shoulders slumped. He didn't know why he kept trying to talk to his mom. She'd gotten worse since his father had died years ago. These days, she judged everyone she saw and everyone came up lacking. He didn't know why he kept trying to keep her in his life. She constantly put him down. He should just let her go and leave his sisters to deal with her.

"So was that all you wanted to tell me? The little trollop from high school fell and you helped her?" His mom yawned into the phone.

Jasper pulled the car into his garage and turned it off. He got out of his car and walked slowly up the steps and opened his door. "Um, yes, I guess that was all. I'll let you go to bed. B-b—"

Click. His mom had hung up. She wasn't much for goodbyes; he should be used to her abrupt disconnects by now. *Why do I keep hoping things will be different?*

Jasper walked down the hall and into his bedroom. He pulled out pajama bottoms and grabbed a towel. He brushed his teeth, got into the shower and turned the water on hot just this side of scalding. It had been a long, but possibly a major turning point of a day, and he needed to get some decent sleep. He relaxed as the water hit him from each of the four showerheads he'd had installed in his primary bath. The extravagant Kohler shower system was worth every penny as it washed away the aches of the day.

Chapter Five

♥

ZAINA

She'd slept with an ice pack wrapped around her leg and as she rolled over and got out of bed, she took it off and bent her knee. The ice pack seemed to do the trick. She felt much better than yesterday and as she walked to her bathroom, she barely limped at all. Now her quads were another story; they were sore from the run.

She looked in the mirror and smiled. She had a secret, and maybe it would be worth it to work with Jasper. Zaina could pretend to date him for a while, if that would mean her dream could come true. Last winter, she'd been manning the counter at her shop when a mother and daughter had come into the store. Zaina thought that the mother was about the same age as her. The little girl was four or five and had on little brown boots and a flowy flowered dress over which she was wearing a cropped jean jacket and she had thick long brown hair in a French braid.

Zaina imagined the mother lovingly braiding her daughter's hair, and suddenly, she felt a pang of yearning. The daughter let go of her mother's hand and started twirling in the front of the store. The late morning sunlight was streaming into her shop window and the little girl's sneakers sparkled in the reflected light. Instead of worrying about something fragile getting knocked over, Zaina resisted the urge to go give the girl a hug. She clenched her fists and walked over to see if the girl's mother needed any help. Normally, Zaina tried not to make assumptions about whether a woman with a child in tow was their parent or not, but the little girl was the spitting image of her mom.

"Welcome to New Age Stones and Witch Crafts. Is there anything I can help you find today?"

The woman was about half a foot taller than Zaina, but most people were taller than Zaina's, five-foot two inches. She was also wearing an empire-waist dress with a jean jacket. Her thick brown hair was -highlighted with golden strands that Zaina was pretty sure resulted from nature and not a talented stylist. She looked over at Zaina and inquired about a tea and honey gift set. She mentioned to Zaina that she was in town to have lunch with an old friend for her birthday. A few minutes later, the mom and daughter had left her store.

That brief interaction changed something in Zaina. Zaina avoided being a living cliché, but even she had to admit, that little girl had caused Zaina's biological clock to stop snoozing. As the days and months had passed over the last year, she'd realized how much she wanted to be a mother and have a child to raise and share her life with, someone to help learn to read and to watch as they learned how to crawl, then walk and then someday to drive a car. Even the idea of having to let that child be out in the world where she wouldn't be able to protect them was something she looked forward to.

There was only one catch, well there were many catches, but the number one issue was her lack of a man. She'd wanted to have a baby so badly she'd convinced herself all the way until the moment Mike had dumped her in October that he was going to propose for Christmas. *Ha!* she thought.

Zaina locked her front door and took the stairs down to her shop. She had an ideal work life; the shop was doing well. She'd finally been able to set up a retirement account. She lived above her shop in a two-bedroom apartment and her stepfather owned the building, so she didn't have to worry about not being able to afford the rent or the building being sold and demolished. Mark hadn't raised her rent since he had fallen for her mother in a whirlwind of a day almost seven years ago.

Zaina turned the sign on the front window to 'open' and then walked over to her tea station to make a cup of tea for herself. She looked at the array of teas lined up for whomever might stop in today. She straightened up the jars, and her hand lingered on the peppermint nettles tea she carried for expectant mothers.

This June, she was going to be thirty-seven. She didn't want to keep waiting for Mr. Right to show up. Every day, she was getting older. If she got pregnant this year, she'd be in her mid-fifties when her baby finished high school. She didn't just want to be a mom; she wanted to see her grandkids. If she tried to do things the organic way, even if she met someone today, and he was the one, it could take years before a baby would be a possibility.

She unlocked the register and checked her cash drawer; it was a force of habit since during the months of January and February, she didn't have a need any part-time staff. This was the time of year when she kept her expenses as low as possible as she watched the funds in her bank account dwindle from the highs of the holiday season. This year was especially bad because of the record cold. She checked the calendar on the wall. Next week was the new moon. Zaina would take the time to do a new moon ritual to manifest some customers.

She sat down behind the counter with her laptop and tea. She clicked on the store's Instagram account and did a double take. Last week, she'd had around nine thousand followers. Today, she had over a hundred thousand followers. She clicked on her notifications and saw that Hop's Heaven had tagged her in a post. She clicked on the link and there was the video from the race. It now had nearly seven hundred thousand views! Maybe Jasper knew what he was talking about.

Zaina opened her ecommerce platform, and her jaw dropped. She had ten new orders! She clicked on each one. None of the new orders were from previous clients or anyone local to her area. Sure, the total of the orders only added up to four hundred and eight-five dollars, but this time of year, every order counted. She pulled out her phone to text Jasper.

> ZAINA: You might be on to something, got some nice orders overnight.

Jasper responded with two emojis, one of the dollar sign eyes and the other of the smiley face, with the tongue sticking out. Three dots pulsed up on her screen again, and she waited to see if he had more to say.

> JASPER: Ready to take things to the next level? #BEERGUYRUNNERGIRL

Zaina looked at her phone screen, then back at her order listing. Even if she had gotten new orders every day for a few weeks, it wasn't enough motivation for her to fake date Jasper. A thought flashed in her mind, and she shivered. "Did fake dating include kissing?" she said out loud.

Her mind flashed back to the homecoming after party. She touched her lips, remembering Jasper's kiss. He had soft lips, and it had been tentative. She'd thought that night was going to be a turning point for her. She hugged herself; it had been a turning point for sure, just not the one she'd expected when they'd shared that sweet kiss. That was before he'd blown her off, starting her decades-long dislike of Jasper.

Was it time to revise her long held hatred? What was in it for her?

She looked back at her phone.

ZAINA: LOL I'm just not there.

JASPER: fair enough. If you change your mind, you have my number.

Zaina sent a thumbs up emoji and put her phone down.

Well, that was that easy. Zaina pressed her lips tight into a grimace. *Why was she feeling a little disappointed?*

The rest of the morning dragged on, and the only one who entered her store was the mail carrier. Zaina felt sluggish, and her legs were still sore from the run. She walked over to the window and noted it was cloudy outside. On the bank marquee across the street from her store, the temperature was a dismal three degrees. Zaina didn't feel like heading upstairs to her apartment for lunch, so she made herself a cup of ramen in the store microwave and slurped noodles in the cozy nook at the front of the store. Once she was warm from the soup, her eyes drooped.

The front doorbell chimed, and Zaina startled.

"Did I catch you sleeping?" Zaina's best friend Nicole unraveled her long scarf and unzipped her coat. She smoothed down her chestnut-colored hair. It was floating around her head like a halo.

"What are you doing here? Shouldn't you be at school?" Zaina asked.

"Dude, it's almost four o'clock."

Zaina smacked her head, "Oh my gosh, I've been asleep for two hours!"

"I heard you wiped out at the race. Maybe you needed the nap to heal?"

Zaina shook her head. "You should have been there. Jasper practically had to drag me across the finish line."

Nicole gave Zaina a little loving shove. "Oh stop, I saw the video. You were a trooper! Don't give him all the credit."

"Speaking of that video, you won't believe what Jasper asked me."

Nicole put her coat, scarf, and gloves on the coat rack by the door and then walked over to make herself a cup of tea. "Do tell," she said over her shoulder.

Once Nicole had doctored her tea to her liking, a little milk and a big squeeze of Acacia honey, she sat down in the yellow armchair across from Zaina. As Nicole slowly sipped her tea, Zaina told Nicole about finishing the race, how Devin and Ben had deserted her when Jasper sat down, and finally she told Nicole about Jasper's proposition for them to fake date.

"Did he say how much he'd pay you to date him?"

Zaina winced. "It sounds terrible when you say it like that."

Nicole played with a gold necklace around her neck.

Zaina leaned in, peering at the gold pendant on the necklace. "Is that a piece of cheese?"

Nicole smiled widely, her eyes lighting up. "Yep, Sean gave it to me on the cruise. He said he tried to find a Denver omelet charm, but no such charm exists."

"Oh, that's right, you two met when he made you an omelet. Y'all are too cute. Have I asked you if Sean has a brother?"

"Yes, you have, and the answer is he has stepbrothers."

"Close enough!" Zaina put up her hand and Nicole high-fived her.

"But seriously, what do you think about Jasper's offer? Did he tell you a dollar amount?"

"Nicole, even if it was ten grand, why would I want to have even a fake relationship with Jasper? You saw how he acted in high school. I'm too old for humiliation."

"I'm not trying to minimize anything, but it has been over twenty years now. People can change."

"He let the entire school think we had sex at the afterparty. Then I came to school on Monday, went to his locker, and he completely ignored me. I wound up with a reputation as a slut." Zaina stood up and tidied their cups. "It still pisses me off. Jasper and the patriarchy still suck."

Nicole got up and gave her friend a hug. "Maybe it's time you used Jasper to your advantage. He was a jerk in high school. Is now the time for him to pay for that?"

"You mean literally pay?"

Nicole nodded, "Exactly, make him pay and make him explain and apologize for his actions in high school."

Zaina retied the belt on her cardigan. "You've definitely given me something to think about. I could use extra funds."

"Is everything okay?" Nicole asked quickly.

"Yes, it's slower than usual for January, but that's just because of the weather. I was thinking about a project I've been considering." Zaina was not ready to tell anyone about her dream of being a mom.

"What's the project? Something for the store?"

"No, nothing business related. Just something I've been thinking about doing. I don't want to talk about it yet."

"If you want to talk about whatever it is, I'm here for you," Nicole said solemnly.

"If I decide to do it, you and Devin will be the first to know."

Nicole smiled, "And if you need any help or feedback on whatever the project is, we are here for you, too."

Zaina nodded. "I know you are. I don't know what I'd do without my best friends."

Nicole's phone chimed. She unlocked it and put it up to her ear. "Hey baby, are you here? I'll be right out."

Zaina walked over to the display window and waved at Sean, Nicole's boyfriend, who was sitting in his Jeep in a parking space in front of the store.

"Do you two have fun plans this evening?"

"We're going out to dinner, which is super rare. Sean says going out to eat feels too much like work for him, but he has a buddy who opened a new restaurant in the city, so we're going to check it out."

"How fun! Have a great time."

Nicole gave Zaina a quick hug. "If you want to talk about Jasper or your project, just text me."

"I will."

Nicole quickly exited the store, and Zaina shivered with the icy blast of air that came in.

She was so lucky not to have to go outside to get to work on days like this. Living above New Age Stones and Witch Craft and being the sole proprietor worked well if she was going to be a single mom. On the downside, she had a high-deductible health insurance plan and needed thousands of dollars before she hit the maximum out of pocket.

Nicole and Jasper's words replayed in her mind. They didn't know she secretly hoped to have a baby, but they both suggested she should consider Jasper's offer. The question was, would he be willing to pay her thousands of dollars for views and likes? It seemed absurd, but that was beside the point. She didn't need to like Jasper or care about his feelings or the ultimate success of his plan, which seemed far-fetched. This was about her getting the funding she needed.

Maybe it would make for a funny story, years from now, when her baby was grown. She rubbed a palm over her heart and continued daydreaming about what could be. Zaina finished printing labels for the online orders she needed to ship and worked on packing up the orders. By the time she was done, the streetlights turned on outside.

She closed the point-of-sale and pulled out her favorite deck of tarot cards; the Modern Witch Deck. Zaina carried the deck over to the reading nook and sat down. She lit a small cone of incense and passed the deck through the smoke. She emptied her mind of business concerns and let her hands hold the cards, slowly shuffling them as she thought about Jasper's proposal. Zaina liked to continue to shuffle the cards for a good long while, it became meditation. The cards passed back and forth between her hands until she felt it was time to ask her question.

She spoke aloud to the cards. "Should I take Jasper up on his offer?" She set the deck down, then she lifted half the deck and put it face down. She pulled the top card off the remaining deck and turned it over. Her breath caught in her throat. It was the judgement card. Time to let go of the past and move forward. She could ignore the card and go on with her life and leave things as they were in her last text with Jasper or she could embrace what judgement represented and see where agreeing to Jasper's potentially crazy scheme took her. She was now ninety-eight percent sure what she was going to do.

Ding Dong!

The door to her shop chimed and in blew the tall, lean form of Jasper.

Chapter Six

JASPER

Hop's Heaven had been pretty dead, so he'd left it in the capable hands of his best bartender, Jax, and drove over to Zaina's shop.

He parked a few doors down from New Age Stones and Witch Crafts and walked over. The wind was blowing, and he regretted not wearing a hat. He only had to walk half a block but by the time he reached her door. His ears were killing him, and the tip of his nose felt ready to fall off.

He pulled open the door to the shop and stomped off his shoes on the floormat.

"Jasper? This is a surprise. How can I help you?"

Jasper tipped his head, pushing the hair off his face. "Do you have anything hot to drink? I'm frozen."

"You came here for a drink?" She squinted in disbelief.

"I was hoping we could talk." He unzipped his coat.

Zaina nodded. "Sure we can talk. I have tea and hot cocoa. Which would you like?"

Jasper felt a warmth of relief upon hearing she would talk to him.

"You can hang up your coat, and then come take a seat," she pointed to her reading area.

"I'll take a tea. As long as it's herbal, I can't do caffeine this late at night." He hung up his coat.

Zaina chuckled.

Jasper felt a pang in his chest. He loved hearing Zaina's sincere laughter, and seeing how her eyes crinkled these days with tiny laugh lines.

"I'm the same way," she said. "Boy, are we getting old."

He folded himself into the low-slung chair and looked at Zaina taking in her long eyelashes, those brown eyes with flecks of gold and her lush red lips. He imagined taking his hand and brushing the back of his fingers along her rosy cheeks and then down to her neck, tilting her head up so he could press his lips against hers. His chest tightened, as he remembered she couldn't stand him.

"You look like you are barely old enough to drink."

Zaina did a little shimmy as she made him a cup of tea. "Honey?" she asked.

"Yes, dear?" He quipped.

She turned, her hand on her hip. "I meant the tea. Did you want some honey in your tea?" She rolled her eyes dramatically.

His grin widened; he loved feisty Zaina. "Oh yes, of course. Please, I can't say no to a little honey."

She added a spoonful of honey to his tea and stirred. "You can't say no to an innuendo either, can you?"

"Actually, I keep so many thoughts in my head."

"So, you aren't just handsome, you've got brains too."

Jasper's pulse beat faster. He hadn't dared imagine flirting with Zaina, but here he was. He felt heat rising on his neck as he watched Zaina carrying the tea over to him. Her hips flared below her slim waist. Her shirt had a deep v, and he knew he could get lost in the view if he wasn't careful.

She leaned down to place a mug rug emblazoned with her shop's logo and as she did; he allowed himself a look, the round swells of her breasts were sprinkled with freckles. What he would give to kiss each of them.

Zaina sat down and Jasper picked up his tea and took a sip.

"Well, what do you think?" She asked, and for a moment, he thought she was asking about his view of her breasts.

"The tea!" he said rather loudly. He stirred his tea and took another sip. "It's good. What kind is it?"

"That one is called Strawberry Shortcake. It's strawberry, obviously, and then it has a little lemon and nutmeg."

"Did you make this?"

"No, I buy it from a girl who makes it locally. Most of the products I sell here are sourced from local vendors, and I sell them on consignment."

Jasper's jaw dropped a little. He had some assumptions about Zaina's little witchy business and this didn't fit with those assumptions. He'd assumed her shop would be a dark, cluttered space with cheap mass-produced fake potions and Ouija boards. He didn't think she'd have a wide array of handmade items from local artisans.

"You look surprised." Zaina squinted at him.

Jasper blushed. "I think you have a savvy business plan. I didn't realize that is what you did."

Zaina shook her head. "If I had to purchase all my inventory outright, I'd never be able to keep this place going."

Here was his opening. "Speaking of opportunities, I didn't come here just to see what you sold."

Zaina nodded. "I didn't think so. Since you've never been in my shop before, I figured there was only one reason you'd show up here in person."

Jasper frowned slightly and gave her his best puppy dog eyes.

Zaina clasped her hands together, "Puppy dog eyes and everything! Sometimes you are too handsome for your own good."

Jasper ran a hand through his hair and smiled. "Is it working?"

Zaina, "Lucky for you, there is something that I want. If you pay me for our viral marketing campaign, and we set some ground rules, yes, I'm in."

Jasper wanted to jump up and give her a hug, but he didn't think she'd react positively to that, so he slapped his hands on his thighs. "This is great, Zaina! What's it going to take? Do you need money to help with your rent? This store must not be cheap to run, especially during the slow season."

"As far as rent goes, I'm lucky. My landlord hasn't raised my rent in years. And if I need any repairs done, he gets someone out here immediately."

Jasper leaned back and stretched out his legs. "You can't beat that. It's rare a landlord doesn't raise the rent. That's one reason I waited until I could purchase the property Hop's Heaven is on."

"There is something else that I'd like funds for."

He cleared his throat. He needed to really play it cool now. "I love that you called my fake dating idea a 'viral marketing campaign' I think that is exactly right. A business arrangement."

Zaina nodded vigorously, "Yes, this isn't personal, just a means to an end."

"So, you're ready to do this?"

Zaina held up a hand, "Provided you'll cover the money I need to reach my insurance deductible and agree to my ground rules."

Jasper swallowed hard. He'd been assuming an offering of a grand would be plenty. This was more than he'd planned on. Then again, if this got him in front of potential investors, it would be a small price to pay. His stomach flip-flopped. Why did Zaina need a bunch of money for medical bills?

"Is that a problem?" Zaina crossed her arms. "I'm not interested in doing it for anything else."

Jasper worried his bottom lip. *Were they really going to do this?* He realized he was at an important crossroads in his life and Zaina would be the catalyst once again. Would things end better this time? His stomach roiled. He might not believe in tarot cards, astrology, or fate, but he couldn't deny the perfect blend of a viral moment with Zaina, and her being able to capitalize on it. Even though it would drain his savings account, he would not let this opportunity pass him by.

"Upcoming medical stuff? Are you okay?" His voice cracked.

"Yes! Everything is great! There is an elective procedure I've been looking into. I just need extra money to pay the bills until I reach my maximum out of pocket, then everything will be covered by the insurance."

He held out his hand. "You've got a deal."

She reached to shake his hand and paused. "We haven't discussed the guidelines for our fake relationship yet."

"Whatever makes you comfortable, I'm happy to agree to."

She pulled back her hand. "Are you sure?"

Jasper put out his hand again, "A hundred percent." His chest tightened with excitement.

"I want half of the money up front."

Jasper nodded, "Fine."

Zaina put her hand in his. He slowly squeezed her soft hand, shaking it. He marveled at how small her hand was in his. She was tiny, but her outsized personality made her seem twice as big.

"So, what are the rules?" He asked.

Let me get my phone.

"Your phone?" Jasper questioned, his brows knitting together.

"I made a note of the terms on my phone."

"Alright then, let's hear it."

"This viral marketing campaign will last a maximum of six weeks. No renewals. One video per week. I approve all videos before they are posted. I'll attend Feel Good Friday at which you may kiss me once. No tongue."

Jasper crossed his arms. "I don't think one kiss during the live remote is enough. We want people to root for us and follow us on social media. Also, I want to get my money's worth." He waggled his eyebrows at Zaina.

"Ew, see, this is exactly why I said no to begin with."

"That came out wrong. What I mean is we need to make this as real as possible for the viewers. Like a scripted reality TV show."

Zaina tapped her phone absently. "How about unlimited light touches on hands, arms or back? Kisses on the cheek when

I give the okay. Hugs as needed, and three on the lips kisses, no tongue."

"How will you give the okay for kisses on the cheek?"

"Hmmm, I'll squeeze your hand."

Jasper nodded. "That should work. What about the hugs as needed? How do we do that?"

"Just don't be obnoxious, and we'll be fine."

"I'll do my best, tall order as that might be."

Zaina's jaw dropped. "My word, is Jasper Kane actually being self-aware? Mark this day on the calendar."

Jasper's cheeks reddened. "Ha-ha, I am an adult."

Zaina held up her hands, "if you say so."

"So, are we good, then?"

"As long as I have the first payment from you before Friday."

Jasper pulled out his wallet and rummaged until he found a folded check. "You got a pen? We can take care of the payment right now."

Zaina went behind the counter and found a pen. Jasper stood at the counter and pulled out his phone. He logged on to his bank account and transferred funds into his checking account. Then he wrote the check, signing his name with a flourish.

"We're really doing this," Zaina said breathlessly.

"We really are," Jasper said, a grin slowing unfolding. He hadn't felt this nervous and excited in a few years. "You know, we should probably get together before Friday and practice."

"Practice what?"

"Liking each other, answering questions Channel Twelve might ask us."

Zaina fiddled with the large gold hoop earrings she was wearing. "I suppose you're right. When do you want to meet up?"

"What time do you close on Thursdays?"

"I close the shop at seven on weeknights."

"Great, we can meet at my house, say eight p.m.? Ideally, we should practice at Hop's Heaven, but I don't think that would be a good idea."

Zaina nodded. "I agree with you. I'd like to have a practice run before we are in front of people."

"Then we are all set! I'll text you my address." Jasper walked over to the coat rack and retrieved his coat and scarf. He put on his coat and wrapped his scarf around his neck. "This is going to be life changing, Zaina. I'm sure of it."

Zaina had a twinkle in her eye as she opened the door for Jasper. "That's my plan."

Jasper turned to look at her, raising his eyebrow. "What do you mean?"

"Nothing to do with you," she assured him. "I have a plan for the money, that's all."

"Alright then, I'll see you on Thursday." He stepped out of the store and heard Zaina lock the door behind him. When he was out of her sight, he allowed himself to do a quick happy dance in recognition of how well the discussion had gone.

Chapter Seven

❤

ZAINA

As soon as she locked the shop door, and Jasper was out of eyesight, Zaina jumped up and down. "I can do artificial insemination!!!" she shouted to the empty shop. She took the check Jasper had written and walked upstairs to her apartment. The only thing that could make this day better was if she could go deposit the check right now. First thing tomorrow she'd finally be able to make an appointment to move forward at the clinic and she'd go deposit this check. Less than two months of fake dating and she'd finally get to have her baby.

She realized it sounded like a Rom Com movie or a limited series on Netflix. "Fake Dating for a Real Baby" or something like that. Would Devin and Nicole think she'd lost her mind? If they did, they might be right. She'd already talked to Nicole and had her full support for this endeavor. Maybe it would be okay to talk about why she was doing this with her best friends. If she was going to make it through these next few weeks, she was going to need their support.

She opened the refrigerator and pulled out a gallon of milk. She put it on the counter, opened her cabinet, and reviewed her cereal choices. Zaina didn't like cooking and had become very good at avoiding it. Plus, after being in her shop all day, the last thing she wanted to do was try to put together a meal. So, cereal it was. She pulled down the box of Peaches and Pecan Oaties then she opened her dishwasher and took out her favorite bowl and spoon. Once the cereal and milk were poured, she put everything back and took her cold dinner to her couch.

Zaina turned on the TV. She started to sit cross-legged but then her knee let her know that was a bad idea. She pulled the coffee table closer and propped up her legs. The TV played in the background as Zaina chewed her cereal. This was how she'd spent almost every evening since Mike had dumped her, but from here on out, that was going to change. No more staying home, being lonely and wishing things were different. The new year was about making changes and growing, and she was ready for that. The first thing she was going to do was FaceTime her best friends and tell them why she was going to be fake dating Jasper. She felt best when she had her friends by her side and if she was going to be a single mom, she'd need them more than ever before.

Zaina unlocked her phone and Facetimed Nicole and Devin.

"Hey Dev, are you busy?" Zaina asked.

"Nicole, how about you? Do you have time to talk?"

Nicole was sitting on her couch. "I'm free. Sean is at work and I was just watching a movie."

"Let me just holler at Ben to take over tonight's reading of *Goodnight, Moon.*"

"The twins still like that book?" Zaina asked.

Devin shrugged as she walked carrying her phone, "It's part of the nighttime ritual. We tried to switch books a few times, and let's just say it didn't end well. Ben! Honey! I'm taking a call with the girls in our bedroom. Take care of the boys!" She walked into her spacious bedroom and flopped on her bed. "What's going on Zaina?"

"Is this about Jasper?" Nicole asked eagerly.

Zaina sat cross-legged on her couch and propped up her phone on the pile of books she had on her coffee table. "No, it's not about him. It's about a decision I've made to start a family."

Nicole gasped.

Devin pursed her lips and nodded. "Tell us more, Z, are you looking to adopt?"

"I'm actually going to pursue artificial insemination."

"I had no idea you wanted to have a baby. How long have you been looking into it?" Nicole had a little furrow between her brows, and Zaina felt her chest tighten.

"Nicole, I'm sorry. Is this baby talk upsetting for you? I feel bad."

Nicole shook her head. "Please, don't worry about me. I'm in a great place in my life. Sean and I are very comfortable being our own family unit and having the time to be the best auntie and uncle to everyone else's kids. I don't begrudge anyone who wants to have children. Don't feel bad!"

"Still, it seems like it's rude to be going on about working to have a baby and you can't have one." Zaina frowned.

"Zaina, if I really wanted to have kids, I could look into fostering or adoption. It's okay for us to want different kinds of families."

Zaina clenched her fist. "Ugh, I should have invited you two over for this conversation so I could hug you right now, Nicole."

"Group hug, girls," Devin said, propping her phone up and then pantomiming a hug.

Zaina and Nicole followed suit.

"Honestly, I started dreaming about having a baby when Mike and I were going strong. I'm not trying to replace him with a baby. I can see where you might think that, but I've been seeing a therapist over the last year and we've been working on why I've spent so many years feeling lonely and lost when I wasn't in a relationship with a man."

"I didn't know you were seeing someone. I am sorry to say I assumed you relied on your tarot cards and your witchy beliefs." Devin hung her head in embarrassment.

"Don't feel bad, Devin!"

Devin made heart hands. "I'm very excited for you, Zaina. I hope you know Nicole and I will drop everything to help you through this process. We can help with appointments, research side effects from the hormones you'll have to take and hold your hand when you take a pee test."

Zaina's eyes teared. "You two are the best!"

Devin and Nicole blew kisses to Zaina.

"Is this why you agreed to fake date Jasper? To help pay for future baby Z?" Devin asked.

"Yep, that's my plan. Please don't tell Sean or Ben. I don't want Jasper to know I'm planning to do artificial insemination."

Devin said, "Of course not!"

Nicole made a 'my lips are sealed' gesture.

"I love you two."

"Love you too!" said Nicole and Devin in unison.

"Night!" Zaina said. Everyone waved good night, and Zaina ended the call.

Her heart was full. She was glad she'd told her best friends why she'd agreed to fake date Jasper. Suddenly, she realized she'd forgotten one condition Jasper had to agree to, or she'd rip up the check. She couldn't believe she'd forgotten to mention it. Zaina put her cereal bowl in the sink and picked up her phone off the counter. She sat back down and texted Jasper.

> ZAINA: I have one more condition.

She hit send and before she put down her phone, she saw three dots. She leaned back and waited for his response.

> JASPER: What's that?

> ZAINA: Since we are 'dating' you can't date or have friends with benefits with anyone else, for the duration of our contract.

He responded right away.

> JASPER: Done.

> ZAINA: Are you sure? We are going to be pretending to be together for nearly two months.

> JASPER: Yes, I'm sure. I'm not going to screw this up and get caught with another woman when I'm fake dating you. I don't want to go viral for being a cheating jerk.

> ZAINA: Good. I'll see you on Thursday.

> JASPER: (thumbs up emoji)

Zaina played absently with her earring. Everything seemed to be squared away now. She didn't know what was going to happen on Friday, but she'd made her decision. It was only eight-thirty p.m. and while the events of the day had been good, she still felt wrung out. She scrolled through the apps on her smart TV until she found the VIKI app, the best app for Asian dramas with accurate English subtitles. She scrolled through until she found "A Business Proposal." If she was going to be part of a real-life fake relationship, she might as well rewatch one of her favorite K-Dramas that had fake dating. She propped up her feet and adjusted the blanket around her and soon she was engrossed in the show.

During episode two, her phone rang, and she saw it was her mom calling. She paused the show and answered her phone.

"Hi, Mom. What's up?"

"Hi honey, I was dropping off Julian at school yesterday and one of the moms showed me this video."

"Was it me finishing the race?"

"It was! You should have told us you were running a race; we could have come out and cheered you on."

"Thanks Mom, really it was no big deal."

"Alright, if you say so," her mom paused, but Zaina knew there was more coming. "Was that Jasper Kane who helped you across the finish line? Did you two make up?"

Zaina rolled her eyes. "Mom, we're grown-ups now. He was the sponsor of the race, so he probably didn't want me to sue him for falling on ice."

"Mm-hmm, that's not what it looks like in that video."

"What do you mean?"

"He might as well have had cartoon hearts around his head when he was singing with you. It was adorable."

Zaina's stomach started churning. She hadn't considered this when she'd agreed to fake date Jasper. Normally, she'd tell her mom she was being silly and that he wasn't her type. If she said that now, how would she explain why she was on TV cozying up to Jasper on Friday? Was it possible to get out of this conversation without lying to her mother? She wasn't ready to explain to her mom, of all people, her deal with Jasper.

"Mom, you will not believe what happened today."

"What honey?"

"Do you watch Channel Twelve's Feed Good Fridays?"

"Of course! We usually have Channel Twelve on in the background on weekday mornings."

"One of the show's producers saw the video of Jasper helping me finish the race and they want to feature Hop's Heaven this Friday. They are going to do a remote live from the brewery!"

"No way! So will you be there too?"

"I wasn't sure if I wanted to be part of it—"

"Oh honey, you have to do it! If it wasn't for you, they wouldn't be doing the remote." Zaina's mom cheered her on.

"Jasper really wants me to be there."

"Mark is out of town, but I'd love to come out on Friday."

Zaina pressed a palm to her forehead. She didn't want Jasper to find out her stepdad was the Mark Anderson, the owner of ADM Investments, the largest venture capital company headquartered in Illinois. He was also her landlord, and she's already made it a point not to mention his existence in her life to

Jasper, knowing how hungry Jasper was for investors. If he met Mark, he'd probably ask him to invest in Hop's Heaven right on the spot. "Don't you have to take Julian to school?"

"I'm sure Monique will watch him. She'll be happy to have a few extra hours."

"Then I guess I'll see you Friday."

"I can't wait! How fun! Maybe this will get you lots of new customers!"

"Thanks Mom."

"I better let you go. Julian needs to go to bed, and I need to text Monique right away. I'm going to set the DVR to record you so Julian can see his big sister on the news!"

"Mom, you're making me nervous."

"You'll be great! Just pretend it's one of the plays you did in high school!"

Zaina laughed, "That's actually brilliant advice, Mom."

"I'm happy I could help! I love you! I'll see you on Friday!"

"Love you too, Mom. See you then!"

Zaina ended the call, pleased it had gone as well as it did. Friday was all about acting, and she'd loved acting in high school.

Chapter Eight

♥

JASPER

Jasper rushed through his house, making sure the bathroom on the main floor was clean. He changed out the hand towels, then went into the kitchen. *What drink pairs well with acting? Do I need snacks?* If this was a regular date and he wanted to impress, he would have ordered an appetizer or two from his best friend Sean's restaurant. This was definitely not a regular date, and he didn't want to give Zaina the impression he was trying to seduce her, so he needed to keep it low key. He thought about the soft slope of her neck and how she had a little mole right below her left earlobe and wished tonight wasn't fake.

He shook his head, and his hair fell on his face. He pushed it back and looked in his refrigerator. As usual, he'd been too busy with work to bother going to the grocery store or putting in a delivery order. He moved bottles of mustard, hot sauce, and pickles around and found a container of hummus. He checked the date, still good. He pulled out the hummus, set it on the counter, and opened his snack drawer. *Perfect.* He had a bag of pita chips. He took out the chips and poured them into a bowl. Then he opened the hummus and put a spoon in it. Jasper carried the snack to his large kitchen island.

He pulled out a bottle of red wine from his wine fridge. If he recalled correctly, the last time he'd seen Zaina at Sean's restaurant with Devin and Nicole, she'd had red wine. He checked the time on his phone. Zaina was going to be here at any minute.

He took a quick whiff under each of his arms; he could be fresher. Jasper took the stairs two at a time to his bedroom. He looked through his closet and found a flannel shirt he knew complimented his broad shoulders and narrow waist. He brought the shirt with him into the adjoining bathroom, put on some deodorant and a spray of palo santo and sage body mist, and changed his shirt.

As he was buttoning it, his doorbell chimed. His mouth went dry, and he rushed downstairs to the door. He opened the door. Zaina smiled, and he stifled a gasp. Usually, when Zaina smiled in his direction, that smile didn't go up to her eyes. Tonight, even her eyes were smiling. "Come on in."

Zaina walked in and pulled off her knit cap. Her short hair stuck up around her head and he couldn't help but smile. She looked so cute with her static-charged hair and rosy cheeks. "You look like you just came in from building a snowman."

Zaina unzipped her coat. "It's so cold, the snow wouldn't stick together."

"Here, let me take your coat."

Zaina handed him her coat and bent to take off her boots.

"Do you want slippers to wear while you're here?"

"Oh," she said, surprised, "that would actually be very nice. Thank you, Jasper."

"No problem. I'll go hang up your coat and grab some slippers. Jasper gestured at the kitchen island. Take a seat and I'll be right back."

Jasper turned away from Zaina, walked over to the closet, and hung up her coat. Warmth filled his chest. *So far. So good.* He pulled out a pair of slippers and carried them over to Zaina.

"Here you go." She put on the slippers; her small feet were engulfed by them. "Sorry I don't have anything smaller."

"Don't apologize. It's sweet of you to offer me any slippers at all."

"I wasn't sure if you were going to be hungry and I didn't have much on hand." He gestured at the hummus and chips.

"I love hummus. This is great."

"What can I get you to drink? I have red wine, or I can get you a seltzer water?"

"This man owns a brewery, and he isn't trying to give me a beer?"

"If you'd like a beer, I've got you covered. I have our Hop's Hefeweizen on tap."

"I'm game. Let me try that. Do you think it will taste good with hummus?"

Jasper nodded. "Yes, in fact, Sean made a beer-infused hummus the other week with the Hefeweizen."

"It's nice that you and Sean can work together."

"He's a great guy."

"I agree, and he's lucky to have Nicole."

Jasper grinned broadly. "Yes, he is." Jasper took out a couple of pint glasses and walked over to his kegerator and poured a couple of pints of beer. He placed the beers on the island and Zaina reached for one of them. "Don't take a drink yet."

"Okay?" Zaina raised an eyebrow.

Jasper opened his refrigerator and pulled open the crisper. Just as he had hoped, he had a lemon. He took it out, then he walked over to his knives and took out a paring knife. He pulled out a bar-sized cutting board and cut the lemon into wedges and garnished Zaina and his glasses.

"There we go," he said, and he walked around to the front of the island and sat down on a stool facing Zaina. "I think you'll like the beer. It has a nice fruity flavor. It tastes nothing like Miller Lite, for example."

Zaina took a sip and her brown eyes lit up. "It's tasty," she said, and she licked the foam off the top of her lip.

Jasper's mouth was dry from watching her tongue sliding over her top lip, so he took a big drink of his beer. "I guess we better get started."

"I can't believe tomorrow we are going to be on TV!" She bounced on her stool.

Jasper took a leap of faith and reached over, wrapping his hand around Zaina's small one. "It's going to be great."

She turned her hand over and entwined her fingers in his. "Your hand is cold," she said.

"Your hand is soft and tiny." He smiled slightly and leaned toward her. Jasper looked from her deep brown eyes rimmed in that black eyeliner she favored and then down to her full lips. He leaned in, wanting nothing more than to feel his lips on hers.

She put a hand on his chest, stopping him. "Jasper, let's focus on what we are going to say tomorrow."

Jasper shook his head, clearing out the fog of desire. "You're right. Sorry about that, it's just—"

"Yes?" Zaina raised an eyebrow.

"You look beautiful."

A flush broke out on Zaina's chest. "I-I, ah, thank you Jasper." She put her hand on his knee.

His chest expanded; she'd taken his compliment. She hadn't made a flippant remark. "If we get lucky, they will just ask us about the race. Maybe they'll ask us about what were singing or something like that."

Zaina played with her chandelier earring. "What if they ask us how we know each other?"

"We both grew up in Marley Creek, and we went to school together." Jasper suggested. His stomach dropped. He was hoping she wouldn't want to talk about how he'd treated her sophomore year.

"What if we just say Marley Creek is our hometown and leave it at that?"

Jasper relaxed. "Great idea!" He took another drink of his beer.

"Do you have a quick elevator pitch for your shop?"

"Yep, I'm all ready for that, thanks to attending the Marley Creek Business Association meetings for over six years now."

"Right. Sorry for assuming you didn't."

"We are going to be on live TV. Better to try and be ready for anything, right?" Zaina tapped his knee.

"Exactly, so let's talk about us."

They went back and forth for the next hour, practicing what they would say when the TV anchors asked them questions. Zaina finished her beer and Jasper got them each a bottle of water. When he caught Zaina yawning, they decided to call it a night.

"Let me get your coat. Are you sure you are okay to drive?"

"Yep, plus the cold air will wake me up." Zaina got up and stretched. As she did, her shirt pulled up and Jasper could see her stomach. He forced down the sudden urge he had to place his hands on her hips and pull her toward him. He clenched his fists and went and retrieved her coat.

Zaina shuffled over to the door in his too big slippers. His heart felt light in her presence.

She took off his slippers and then put on her boots. He held up her coat. As she put it on, he breathed in the scent of her; she smelled like honey and mint. She turned and zipped up her coat.

"Sweet dreams, Jasper."

"Hug goodnight?"

"Yes, why not? We might as well practice that for tomorrow too."

Jasper's heart dropped a little. He'd almost forgotten this was a charade. *Get it together, Jasper!*

"Come here," he said and opened his arms wide.

Zaina nestled herself in his embrace. He gave her a squeeze and she pulled back but stayed in his arms. He put his finger under her chin, tilting her head up. She looked up into his eyes and he bent his head down. "Should we practice a kiss?"

"Sure," she said with a half-smile.

He leaned in, closing his eyes, eager to taste her. And his lips brushed against her cheek.

His eyes flew open, and she was grinning from ear to ear, joy dancing in her eyes.

He shook his head. "You got me that time."

She raised her arms above her head like a prizefighter. He continued shaking his head. He couldn't be mad; he was just happy she was having fun with this. "If you can bring this level of fun tomorrow, we are going to nail it!"

She gave him another quick hug and before he could react, she opened the door to leave.

"See you soon!" she said as she walked down his steps.

"Text me so I know you made it home!"

She gave Jasper a thumbs up and finished walking to her car.

He sighed and closed the door. Tomorrow was the big day; he needed to get some sleep.

Chapter Nine

♥

ZAINA

She'd set her alarm for four-thirty, but she'd barely slept a wink in anticipation of the morning show. Not only was she going to be on the top morning show in Chicago, but she was also going to be acting! She'd never been able to sleep the night before a performance in high school, and this was going to be the biggest performance of her life. Plus, it had been decades since she had acted.

She hopped out of bed and made a big cup of coffee. Then she took a shower and used eye serum, eye cream and under eye concealer to hide the circles from lack of sleep. It would be amazing if there was a makeup artist at the shoot that might freshen up her face, but she doubted that would happen.

Zaina sat at her vanity and carefully made up her face. She typically wore her version of grown-up goth, which meant she went heavy on the eyeliner and preferred plum lip colors. Today she followed a YouTube tutorial she'd found for how to look your best on camera. She carefully followed the instructions and ten minutes later, she was so thrilled with how she looked, she snapped a selfie and sent it to Devin and Nicole. Then she remembered it wasn't even five a.m. yet. *Well, they'd see it when they got up.*

She smiled at herself and put on her favorite earrings. They were handmade by a local artisan and were sterling silver cascading tear drops. She shook her head, and they tinkled as the teardrops bounced against each other. She took off her robe and put on her favorite pair of jeans and a royal blue top with ruching. Zaina checked the temperature on her app; finally, the temperature was in the teens. She didn't know how cold it might be in the brewery and she was usually cold, so she put on a pair of knee-high fuzzy socks and made her way to her kitchen. Her stomach was swirling with butterflies. She didn't feel hungry at all, but she knew she had better try to eat something before she left for the brewery. Zaina pulled out a cup of vanilla Greek yogurt and a package of black raspberries. She mixed the raspberries in to the yogurt and stood at her kitchen counter eating. Her phone chimed.

JASPER: (photos attached.) Which shirt should I wear?

ZAINA: Good morning to you too! You're not wearing Hops Heaven merch?

JASPER: Should I?

ZAINA: The rest of the staff will have on their logo shirts, right?

JASPER: Yep.

ZAINA: Then no, you want to stand out as the owner.

JASPER: Thanks Z.

ZAINA: Calling me Z isn't part of our agreement.

JASPER: Sorry. Okay Zaina, which shirt?

ZAINA: I'm wearing a royal blue shirt if that helps.

JASPER: I'll wear the orange plaid flannel.

ZAINA: A man who knows his complementary colors, I am impressed.

JASPER: I took some art classes in college. They come in handy when I'm working on marketing for the brewery.

ZAINA: Makes perfect sense. I'll be in blue, representing calm, peaceful and professional vibes and you'll be in orange, giving fun, playful creative vibes. That's actually brilliant, Jasper.

JASPER: (blushing face emoji) Thanks...Z.

ZAINA: Fine! You can call me Z!

JASPER: (high five emoji)

ZAINA: I've gotta run and do my lipstick. I'll see you soon.

JASPER: Same!

ZAINA: (LOL emoji)

Zaina finished eating, brushed her teeth, and put on some extra deodorant, just in case. She applied her lip primer, lip liner, and lipstick. She started her car from the upstairs window and put on her long puffer coat. She pulled the hood up, and carefully wrapped her lucky scarf around her face. She locked the door behind her and skipped down the stairs. Zaina didn't need to pull a tarot card to know today was a day that would change the rest of her life.

She turned into the parking lot of Hop's Heaven at a quarter after five. The TV trucks were already there. A large antenna truck was inside an area cordoned off with traffic cones. Zaina maneuvered her car to the back of the parking lot and parked. Her breathing was shallow and she could feel her heart beating in her ears. Before she went inside, she needed to calm down. She sat in her car for a minute, just to take a couple of deep breaths. This was just another stage and she'd been on plenty of them. After a minute, Zaina was ready to go inside.

She got out of her car and rushed to the brewery door. She walked inside to the already busy scene. Jasper must have everyone from his staff working this morning. The front of the taproom was transformed for the broadcast. Lighting had been placed around a grouping of two high top tables and chairs. Unwinding her scarf from around her head, she scanned the room for Jasper but didn't see him. A camera man walked in behind her and grunted, so she got out of the way and walked over to where Nicole's boyfriend, Sean, was setting up a buffet.

"Hi, Sean!" she said unzipping her coat.

Sean smiled, showing off those dimples everyone, especially Nicole loved. "Zaina, you look fantastic! I'd give you a hug, but I don't want to mess you up."

"Aww, thank you, Sean! You look great too!"

Sean pushed out his chest and preened. His broad shoulders and chest filled his chef's jacket. "Thanks, Zaina. Nicole gave me her approval before I left the house. She even tidied up the back of my hair last night since I didn't have time for a haircut." He turned around. "What do you think?"

Zaina stood on her tiptoes. "Looks great, Sean. Is Nicole here?"

"I woke her up to make sure I looked okay before I left, and she fell right back asleep. You know how she is in the morning."

Zaina burst out laughing. "I sure do!"

"Right, so she'll be here by seven."

Zaina nodded. "I better let you get back to setting up the food. It smells amazing, as usual!"

"Thanks, make sure you come eat some!"

She looked around again for Jasper, and this time, she saw him speaking to someone who must have been with the television crew.

"Zaina," said Sean.

Zaina turned back toward Sean.

"Do you want to put your coat and stuff back here, or you could go put it in Jasper's office? I know he has a coat rack in there."

"Thanks, Sean. I'll go put it in his office."

Zaina turned to the left and walked past the bar and into Jasper's office. Ethan, Sean's stepbrother and Jasper's latest bar-back and general clean up guy was sitting in a chair nodding off. Zaina smiled. He was a cutie. She tip-toed past him and hung up her coat, then as she began putting her scarf over her coat, someone grabbed her waist. She shrieked and fell back against the hard muscled chest of Jasper. He chuckled into her ear. "Did I catch you off guard?"

She breathed in the palo santo and sage scent she associated with Jasper and allowed herself to notice that her immediate reaction to his silliness was not to turn around and push him away. Was she in the acting zone or was her heart softening? A flush began creeping up her neck. Jasper's hands were on her waist and she was pressed against him. He pushed her slightly away from him and she got her footing.

"What the heck! I was trying to grab a little nap," Ethan said, and he stalked out of the room.

"He shouldn't be in here napping anyway. Thanks for waking him up, Z."

Zaina adjusted her shirt. "What time is it? How soon does it start?"

Jasper tossed his hair. I was talking to the production manager, and he said we go live at seven after six. He pulled out his phone and looked at it. "We have twenty minutes."

Zaina rubbed her suddenly sweaty palms on her jeans. "How do I look?"

Jasper gave her a slow wolf whistle. "Zaina, you look so hot." His eyes blazed as he looked her up and down and then into her eyes.

The flush that had started on her neck rose until her entire face was flaming red. She fanned herself, "Don't make me blush, Jasper!"

"I can't help it, Zaina. You're gorgeous."

She played with her earring at a loss for words. The air between them was thick with desire.

He reached out and took her hand in his. "Let's go talk to the production people. I want to introduce you."

She swallowed and took his hand. "Sounds great, let's go."

The next twenty minutes passed in a flash. The taproom was filled to capacity. A line had formed for Sean's buffet. Zaina was introduced to several members of the staff from Channel Twelve as well as some of Jasper's staff. She'd already forgotten half of their names in her nervousness. She was grateful she'd been able to stick close to Jasper. He was laying on the charm today, and she finally understood why people, especially women, were drawn to him. He had an effortless charm, and that made you want to be around him, and he was goofy often enough to remind you he was human. She watched as he glad-handed the local business owners who had decided to come to the remote broadcast.

The morning television crew was seated at a high-top table. The Hop's Heaven neon logo featured prominently behind them. Zaina was sure that Jasper had lobbied hard to make sure the logo would be visible during the broadcast. A makeup artist was putting the finishing touches on the sports guy and the weather girl was getting help with her mic.

Zaina felt detached from the surrounding scene. It was almost like she was in a dream and then suddenly the production manager yelled, "We're live in twenty!" Over the PA system, a countdown began. Zaina looked around the room for Jasper and saw Devin walking in the front door. She rushed over to her friend.

"Devin, I'm so glad you're here!"

Devin gave Zaina a very careful hug, "Even if I wasn't the mayor, I wouldn't miss this for the world. How are you doing?" She held Zaina's hand. "Your hand is freezing."

"I'm so nervous!"

"You look amazing. If it helps, you don't look nervous at all."

"Thank you, Dev. Hey, I don't think there are any seats left, but you can put your coat and stuff in Jasper's office."

"That would be great, hon. I'm not on until the eight o'clock hour. I just came early to see you."

Zaina gave her friend a squeeze and Devin went to hang up her coat. Zaina watched as the news crew began their morning greetings. Suzy Snow was a petite Black woman who did the weather. Jake Boreman was a burly red head that did the sports. Chrissy White was an older woman and the senior news anchor. She'd been on Channel Twelve since Zaina was a kid and John Johnson was the new male anchor. He sported a shaved head, and that just brought more attention to his gorgeous smile.

With each passing second, she got more nervous. She took a deep breath and held it, then slowly let it out and as she took a second breath, she breathed in his scent, and she knew Jasper was right beside her. He put his hands on her shoulders and lightly massaged.

"Your shoulders were around your ears, so I thought I'd come see if I could help."

"Thank you. I'm so nervous. I don't know why. I used to go on stage all the time."

"I'm nervous too," he reassured her. "Remember when they cue up the video of us finishing the race, we need to go sit at the table next to the morning crew." He stopped massaging her shoulders, but he kept his hands on her shoulders, and she let herself enjoy how his touch helped ground her. Then she heard the news crew talking up their viral moment. Jasper reached out his hand and she took it, letting him lead the way over to the high top table next to the news anchors. On the table was a microphone, so neither Zaina nor Jasper had to wear mic packs.

Jasper pulled out her chair and she stepped up and sat on the bar stool. Her short legs dangled far from the ground. He pushed in her chair and then sat down on the edge of his chair; his long legs planted firmly on the ground. Just out of camera range, Jax, the lead bartender at Hop's Heaven, stood with a pitcher of Jasper's new sessions IPA, a lower alcohol beer suitable for the morning.

As the video was finishing, Jasper leaned over and whispered in Zaina's ear, "Do it like we practiced."

That was her cue. She smiled and laughed and the camera caught it all.

John Johnson began speaking, "It's another fabulous Feel Good Friday here in Chicagoland! What you just watched was the heartwarming viral video showing Jasper Kane, owner of Hop's Heaven Brewery, here in beautiful Marley Creek and Zaina Evans, the runner who fell down, but didn't stay down thanks to Jasper! Thanks so much for having us out today and for spending your morning with us."

He turned toward his co-anchor Chrissy White, who began speaking, "Yes, we are thrilled to get this opportunity to meet the pair behind this inspirational viral video. Zaina, can you tell us how you were feeling when you fell?"

Zaina smiled and sat up straighter. Under the table, Jasper reached over and squeezed her hand. She tried not to think about how sweaty her hands were. "Thanks for asking, Chrissy. I was so frustrated when I fell. It was super cold outside, and I was almost finished! Then suddenly, splat! I was on the ground!"

"I think we've all been there. I don't run, but I have slipped on ice and that is no fun. Fortunately, we will see a warm up soon and I'll be talking about that at twelve past the hour," said meteorologist, Suzy Snow.

"Jasper, why did you decide to run out and help Zaina finish the race? Were you friends?" Chrissy asked.

"Marley Creek is our hometown. We went to school together, but no, we weren't friends. I was at the finish line helping to hand out finisher medals. I saw Zaina fall and," he shrugged his shoulder, "I didn't even think. I just ran out to where she was."

"When you saw a big beer mug making its way toward you, what did you think, Zaina?"

"Honestly?" She looked at Jasper sideways, "I was like, who the heck is that?"

Jasper dropped his jaw in pretend shock. "You didn't recognize me?"

Zaina playfully pushed him. "I had just fallen flat on my face. I'm lucky I didn't get a concussion."

"Whose idea was it to start singing?" John Johnson asked.

"We have Ethan to thank for that. Where are you, Ethan?" said Jasper.

Ethan rushed up from the behind the bar and came over to the table. He waved at the camera.

"Ethan, why did you start playing 'Eye of the Tiger'"? Jake Boreman asked.

Ethan leaned in between Zaina and Jasper so he was closer to the microphone and said, "Jake, is it even a sporting event if they don't play 'Eye of the Tiger'?"

Jake erupted with a belly laugh and replied, "So true Ethan, so true!"

Chrissy White asked, "Zaina, so how did you feel when you found out you'd gone viral?"

Zaina smiled broadly and widened her eyes, "I didn't believe it at first! And then I was nervous. What were people saying?"

Suzy Snow chimed in, "They were saying y'all look like you'd make a cute couple!"

Applause broke out in the taproom.

"We have to know. Are you single Jasper?" asked John Johnson with a raised eyebrow.

"I am," replied Jasper.

"And how about you, Zaina, seeing anyone special?" Chrissy White queried.

"Well, actually..."

"Oh, no!" groaned Jake Boreman.

"Let her finish," Suzy Snow chided.

"Jasper and I are going on a date!" Zaina's eyes lit up with delight. She leaned toward Jasper and he wrapped his arm around her.

"I guess when Zaina fell, well, sparks flew!" gushed Chrissy White.

"After the race, we got to talking, and I asked if she'd like to go on a date with me. Not gonna lie, I was shaking in my boots, afraid she was going to say no, but she said yes!"

The audience and the crew said, "Aww."

"Talk about a Feel Good Friday! Will Jasper and Zaina fall for each other? Or will this couple run out of steam before the finish line? And how are the roads looking out there? We'll be back after traffic on the twos," John Johnson announced.

Make-up and hair personnel ran over to the morning crew and began fixing fly away hairs and make-up smudges.

The production manager walked over to Zaina and Jasper, "You two are doing a fantastic job! The comments on the livestream are blowing up. People want to know more about your date."

"This is wild," Zaina said.

"We always have high viewer engagement for Feel Good Fridays, but this is like, beyond. Keep doing what you're doing, and Jasper, we'll kick off the next segment with your beer."

Jasper nodded, and the production manager jogged off to go talk to John Johnson.

Chapter Ten

♥

JASPER

Jasper tapped on his leg, anxiously waiting for the traffic and weather segments to be done. The live remote with Channel Twelve could not have been going any better. The only thing that could make this day better would be if an investor would walk thru the door and offer him a contract to take Hop's Heaven nationwide. Jasper let himself daydream about what that first meeting would be like and then the show was going to commercial.

"Jasper, my mom just came in. I'm going to go say hi to her." Zaina waved at her mom, who was in the very back of the room.

Jasper followed Zaina's wave and saw a slim woman with long dark brown hair. She was taller than her daughter, but Zaina was the spitting image of her mother. "Let me go with you. I'd love to meet her."

Zaina tilted her head and looked at Jasper. "You would?"

"Yes, of course. We're going on a date. I should like to say hello."

"I mean, it's not the nineteen fifties, and we are well into our thirties, but alright, let's go."

Jasper followed Zaina as she wound her way through the tables and all the people standing until they got to Zaina's mother. Zaina and her mom began hugging. Up close, Zaina's mom looked even younger. Jasper waited as they rocked back and forth hugging.

"Thanks for coming out, mom!"

"I wouldn't miss it! You are doing great!"

"You're making me blush." Zaina turned to Jasper, "Jasper, this is my mom, Amy."

"It's a real pleasure to meet you, Ma'am."

"Just call me Amy! It's wonderful to meet you, Jasper. Now, did I hear you two are going on a date?"

Zaina and Jasper looked at each other. Zaina gave him a small nod and he began speaking. "Do I have your permission to date your daughter?"

Amy smiled and laughed, "You are quite the charmer, Jasper! Zaina is old enough to date whomever she chooses. I will say, I think we are all so invested in your date, you might need to live-stream it. You'd have more people watching your date than the Bears this year.

"Zaina rolled her eyes. "Mom, you're so dramatic."

"Twenty seconds, people!"

"I have to get back up front, Zaina." Jasper said.

"I'll stay back here with my mom."

"Nice to meet you, Jasper," Amy said and then she surprised Jasper by giving him a hug. He wasn't used to parent hugs, not from his own parents, and especially not from someone he was dating. His throat felt tight. He didn't have time to be mushy right now. It was time to let the world, and most importantly any potential investors in the tri-state area know all about his baby, Hop's Heaven.

"Now that it's after eight o'clock, it's got to be noon somewhere, right? And we can't have a Feel Good Friday at a brewery and not taste what they serve! Jasper Kane, please tell us what we have here."

The camera turned to Jasper, who was holding a pitcher of beer.

"Here at Hop's Heaven, whether it's a football game on a Sunday morning or Saturday afternoon with friends around the grill, we've got you covered with our new sessions IPA, The Post Run."

"What's a sessions IPA?" asked Suzy Snow.

"Thanks for that question! It's an IPA, which is a beer that has lots of hops to give it a signature citrus flavor, but instead of having a higher alcohol content, it has less, so you can enjoy it over a nice long afternoon session."

"I love that!" chimed in Chrissy White.

Jasper carefully poured and served each member of the morning crew. Originally, the production manager had suggested that one of his staff do the pouring while he talked, but Jasper recognized it would look better and have more of an impact if he served.

John Johnson took a drink and then asked, "This is very refreshing! Why did you name it, The Post Run?"

"I wanted to make a special beer that everyone who took part in the Frosty Toes 10K could enjoy, and I knew it should be a lighter beer, but still delicious. So, I came up with this beer and I thought The Post Run was the perfect name."

"I think that's exactly right. I might go for a run if I could come home and have one of these! Does this come in cans?" Jake Boreman asked.

"We have crowlers, which are 24 oz cans we fill on demand. But who knows, maybe someday soon there will be more Hop's Heavens."

"That sounds like a plan to me, and speaking of plans, after this commercial break, we'll be talking to the mayor of Marley Creek, Devin Belmont about why your next staycation should include a day trip to Marley Creek."

Jasper walked over to the buffet. "Thanks again for coming out, Sean."

Sean came out from around the buffet and gave Jasper a hug. "I wouldn't miss this for anything! What a great crowd."

"To be far, people are always happy when there's free food."

"True, and today there's even free beer!" Sean laughed.

"One, one free beer per guest." Jasper quipped.

Jasper slapped his friend's back. "Thanks again, man!"

"You and Zaina look like you are having a great time up there."

"I've got to say, she makes it easy for me to smile."

"You get a really goofy look on your face when you say her name." Sean peered dramatically into his friend's eyes. "I think she might be the one."

"The one? P-please, phhhhh." Jasper waved his hand. "There's no such thing."

"Feel free to keep denying it and I'll just save this moment for my best man's speech at your wedding."

Jasper shook his head dismissively. "You know what the deal is, Sean. We're just acting."

"Oh yes, acting. Nicole told me all about the plan. But I think there's something else going on."

"Sean, it's been great. I think I'm needed back on the set. I'll talk to you later. I'll be right there!" Jasper said to no one in particular.

Sean smiled and shook his head. Jasper started walking toward the front of the room. He saw Zaina was talking to Nicole, so he made a detour over to her. Zaina looked up, and Jasper put his arm around her. "Is this okay?" He whispered in her ear. She nodded and he gave her a squeeze. She felt so good in his arms. She felt right. Were they just acting? He knew he was lying to himself. This was no act on his part. He'd been pining for her for years.

"Nicole, thanks for coming out." Jasper said.

"I have to support my girl!" Nicole tipped her auburns curls toward Zaina.

Zaina high-fived her friend, "Support each other, that's what we do."

"Speaking of, where's Devin?" Zaina asked.

"I think she's trying to talk the product manager into coming back to Marley Creek to do a show for the Marley Creek marathon." Jasper nodded with his head toward where Devin was talking with her hands to the production manager.

"That would be brilliant!" Zaina said.

"Zaina, you should run the marathon this year!" Nicole said enthusiastically.

"Whoa, whoa, whoa, slow your roll. I barely managed the 10k."

"I'm sure if you put your mind to it, you'd be able to run the marathon with no problem," Jasper offered.

"Aww! Way to be supportive, Jasper!" Nicole said, and she gave Zaina a knowing look.

Zaina looked taken aback. Jasper wasn't sure what that was about. "I hope I didn't offend you Zaina, I'm just saying you've got that can-do-spirit."

Zaina's eyes looked a little glassy, and her voice dropped as she answered, "No, you didn't offend me. Not at all."

She looked away from Jasper.

At the front of the room, the countdown to going live had started. "We better get back up there, Zaina." Jasper said.

Zaina squeezed her friend's hand, and then Jasper and Zaina walked back to their table for their final segment.

"Thanks for that update on the potential for a winter storm next week! Any chance we'll see substantial snow, Suzy?"

"Right now, there is a potential for a significant ice storm event. We could also see snow," Suzy Snow replied.

"I don't like the sound of that. Everyone make sure you get prepared this week for a loss of electricity if that ice storm shows up!" John Johnson said.

"And speaking of electricity, We've been getting so many questions on our live stream about Jasper and Zaina. Everyone wants to know more about your date! Tell us the details you two!" Chrissy White said.

Jasper's hands were suddenly sweaty. Things had gotten real. He carefully rubbed his hand on his jeans and he put his hand out and Zaina slipped hers in his. Her small hand was clammy and instead of grossing him out, it made him feel better.

Jasper nodded at Zaina and she began speaking. "Oh my gosh, talk about pressure! We're planning to go out next Friday, and no, we aren't going to live stream our date!"

"Oh bummer! No fan cam?" said Suzy Snow.

Zaina threw her head back and laughed, "No thank you!"

Jasper chimed in, "But we need to think about our fans, Zaina!"

"That is true, Jasp. What should we do?

"Aww, she called him Jasp," said Chrissy White.

"If you follow the Hop's Heaven account on any of our socials, we're going to post outtakes from our date."

"How fun! Will there be singing?" said Jake Boreman.

Jasper and Zaina looked at each other and laughed. "Maybe?" they said in unison.

"There you go, everyone. You can't go on the date with them, but you can follow the antics of Jasper and Zaina next week on the Hop's Heaven socials, and if you are in the mood for a tasty homegrown beer come on out to Hop's Heaven in Marley Creek. They are open seven days a week from eleven a.m. to eleven p.m. Wave to the folks at home, Jasper and Zaina!" John Johnson said.

Zaina tapped Jasper's leg, and he leaned over and kissed the crown of her head. Relief flooded through him. Their practice session had paid off. The live remote couldn't have gone better. Now he just needed to figure out how to turn this publicity into investor interest and pull off a great date. Maybe they needed to google viral date moments for inspiration.

The television crew quickly began closing and packing up all their equipment. Chrissy White had given Zaina and Jasper a big hug and signed head shots of all four members of the morning crew. Jasper made a mental note to hang up the autographed pictures behind the bar. He'd recorded the show on the brewery's DVR and he planned to run the episode on a loop over the weekend on the TVs when football wasn't on.

Sean had packed up his buffet and left to get back to his restaurant and most of the crowd, except a few tables, had also left. Zaina looked antsy as she stood next to the bar.

"You probably need to head over to your shop?" Jasper asked.

"Yes, I've got an oil making class this afternoon to prep for."

"Oil making class, what's that about?"

"We mix a carrier oil like almond oil or coconut oil with different essential oils for specific purposes and you can use the oil to dress candles that you use when doing rituals, which are like a prayer. You can also use the oil on your pulse points to boost mood, for example."

"Sounds too woo-woo for me, but thanks for explaining."

"It's not for everyone," Zaina acknowledged. "I appreciate you not making fun of my work."

"I wouldn't make fun of you. You have a passion for what you do and people love your shop, so what do I know?" He shrugged, "Though I wonder—"

"Yes?"

"Can my pet name for you be Witchy Poo?"

"Absolutely not."

"Wait, I'm giving you my puppy dog eyes. Women can't resist this face, please?"

"Guess what, big guy?"

"What, Witchy—"

Zaina clapped her hand over his mouth. "I'm immune to your face! You can call me Zaina, Z or Ms. Evans!"

"Gowth it."

"What was that?" She removed her hand.

"Got it."

"Now if you want to call me Big Guy, you go ahead. Feel free, I like it."

"Let's see how things go on Friday." She patted his cheek and then turned and walked to get her coat from his office.

Jasper was behind the bar when she came out of his office, bundled up to leave. "I'll see you on Friday, Ms. Evans!"

"Yes, you will, Jasp!"

She swept out of the brewery and the door swished behind her.

At the bar, an older woman with her laptop in front of her and a glass of water at her side let out a low whistle and said, "My goodness. What are you up to, Jasper?"

"Nothing, Kathy, just living the good life. You know me!"

Kathy pulled down her reading glasses and eyeballed Jasper, "That's why I'm asking what you are up to."

"Kathy, I think your writer's imagination is leading you astray. Why would I be up to anything?"

Kathy pointed at Jasper, "That is an excellent question. I don't know why, I just know you are up to something. I hope Zaina is in on it with you. She's a good kid. Don't break her heart."

Jasper shook his head. "What about my heart, Kathy?" he asked, mostly facetiously.

"Oh Jasper, you are such a flirt." Kathy shook her head and went back to typing on her laptop. "Just remember, I'm here if you want to talk. Maybe I can help. I write kissing books."

Jasper poured himself a glass of water and took a drink. "Kissing books? That's what you're calling them now?" He pointed between them, "We both know there is a lot more than kissing going on in your books."

"You're missing the point, Jasper. My books are about love. It's about people who have a hole in their hearts and they meet another person who makes them whole. That's what the happily ever after is all about."

Jasper felt a lump in his throat. Why had the image of Zaina laughing flooded his mind when Kathy was talking about romance? He must be more tired than he thought. He cleared his throat. "Thanks, Kathy. I'm going to my office to work on some paperwork."

Kathy put her glasses back on and began typing. "Have a good nap, Jasper."

"I can't pull one over on you," Jasper shook his head.

"It comes from being a nosy writer!" she joked as Jasper walked toward his office. He was ready for a nap before the afternoon crowd came in later today.

Chapter Eleven

♥

ZAINA

Zaina buzzed in Nicole and listened as she clomped up the stairs to Zaina's apartment.

"I shouldn't have worn these boots, but they said we might get snow today, so I thought I better wear my space boots." Zaina opened the door wide for Nicole, who stopped at her door mat and took off her calf-high silver moon boots.

"Where did you even get those things?" Zaina laughed.

Nicole took off her Ida B. Wells Elementary Eagles cap and stuffed it into her long puffer jacket pocket. She smoothed her wavy auburn locks and took off her coat and walked into Zaina's house.

"Sean got them for me as a white elephant Christmas present, but I showed him. I'm wearing them every time they call for snow." She sat down on Zaina's couch and put her legs under her.

Zaina went into the kitchen. Her apartment was an open concept with just a low row of cabinets separating the kitchen from the living room. "The pizza should be here in about twenty minutes. What do you want to drink? Would you like a glass of wine or a beer or Coke?"

"I'll take a glass of wine. I know you're supposed to have red wine with Italian food, but half the time, red gives me a headache, so I'll take a glass of white."

"Coming right up." Zaina poured two glasses of white wine and brought them over to the table. "You two are so cute. I know you've been together less than six months, but do you think he is going to propose?"

Nicole twisted a lock of her hair. "We have talked about plans for the future, but we haven't really talked much about getting married."

"It's going to happen, Nicole! I bet by this time next year you'll be Mrs. Harper."

"Maybe I'll keep my name. I've had it for over thirty years."

"Maybe he'll take your name?"

"Sure, why not? Why are we always being asked to give up our names? It's time for the men to give up theirs!"

Zaina raised her glass, and Nicole did as well. "A toast to changing norms!" They clinked their glasses and each took a drink. Zaina checked her watch. "The pizza will be here in a few. After we eat, I'll show you what I'm planning to wear for the date tomorrow."

"I can't wait! What are you guys going to do?"

"Jasper ordered a meal from Sean, and we are going to hang out at Hop's Heaven."

"You're not going somewhere romantic?"

"I think it's more about product placement. You know, this is a business venture for him. And for me too, of course!"

"Ya, I get that. Still, it seems like a bit of a bummer."

"I think it will take some of the pressure off me. I won't start thinking swoony thoughts about Jasper." Zaina explained.

"He is pretty swoon worthy, isn't he? Those brown eyes, his chiseled face, the broad shoulders and the taper of that man's waist. I bet his obliques are cut! If I wasn't so head over heels for Sean, I might want to take a ride on the Jasper Kane express. You could climb him like a beanpole, and I bet he'd like that too."

Zaina's face was beet red by the time Nicole finished going on about Zaina's fake boyfriend.

Buzz!

"Pizza's here!" Zaina jumped up and rushed to the door. She pressed the intercom button. "I'll come down and get it."

Nicole got up and brushed off her pants. "I'll get plates and napkins."

"Thanks, hon," Zaina said, and she slid her feet into the slippers she kept at her door and ran downstairs to get the pizza.

Within a couple of minutes, they were sitting at Zaina's kitchen table enjoying tavern-style cheese and mushroom pizza.

"There is something about a hot pizza on a cold winter night that always hits the spot. Did you get double dough?"

"Yes, I always get double dough when I order from Best Pizza Near Me."

"It's fantastic. Not too much dough, just the right amount."

"Mm-hmm," Zaina said, her mouth full of pizza.

A short time later, they had made a big dent in the pizza and Zaina was wrapping up a few pieces for Nicole to take home to Sean.

"Zaina, I know you said you're only doing this for the money, but are you sure that's all there is to this? You two look like you were having so much fun at the remote and Jasper's eyes were fixed on you the whole time."

Zaina's stomach flip-flopped. "We practiced the night before the broadcast, so we were prepared to look like a couple. That's what you must have seen. And for this date, we'll post some videos that also show us looking like we're really into each other, but it's just acting."

Nicole squinted at her friend. "Just acting? Are you sure that's what you're going with? It's me here, Z."

Zaina sighed, "Okay, fine. Yes, he's gorgeous and there's something vulnerable about him that makes me want to give him a hug and make it all better."

"So why not just tell him that? Zaina, I swear, he is into you. He's more into you than you think—by far!"

"I can't. I can't trust him. He hurt me in high school, and I can't get past it."

"Have you asked him why he did it or if he is sorry?"

"Nicole, should I have to ask him why? If there was a *good* reason, wouldn't he have told me by now?"

"I don't know, Z. I just know what I see, and I see two people who are very into each other. What if you just think about it, and if high school comes up at all, ask him about it—or just tell him how he hurt you, then go from there. Maybe he will surprise you. Perhaps something good can come out of your fake relationship."

Zaina reached over and held her friend's hand. "Thank you, Nic. You give fantastic advice, even when I don't know that I want to follow it." Zaina smiled a crooked smile.

"I'm always here for you, Z." Nicole patted Zaina's hand. "Now on to the fun stuff. Show me your date outfit!"

Zaina hopped up, "I got a new dress. It's plum. Hang on, let me go get dressed. Do you want some wine while you wait?"

Nicole held up her glass. "Yes, please!"

Zaina poured some wine in each of their glasses and then she went to her bedroom to change. She pulled on a pair of black patterned tights and a lacey push-up bra and she stepped into her cashmere plum colored dress. It clung to her curves and accented her breasts; the dress stopped mid-thigh. She'd splurged on this dress because her mom and Mark had given her a gift card for Nordstroms Department Store and she'd decided the best thing to do was not to say, "Oh this is too much," as she was inclined to do. Instead, she'd used the gift card to buy an investment piece. The dress was a classic winter style, and she could wear it for years. Someday, she might even pass it on to her daughter, if she had a daughter.

She looked at the boots in her closet and put on one knee-high stiletto heeled boot and on the other foot, she put on her favorite shoes, her shiny black Dr. Martens. She smoothed down her dress and fluffed up her short hair, giving it a soft swoosh to the side instead of wearing it spiky. To top off her look, she put on purple passion lipstick, which wasn't as purple as the name suggested.

"I'm coming out. Let me know which boots I should wear."

Zaina sashayed down the hall doing a runway walk, then stopped and turned for her friend.

She put her hand on her hip, looked at Nicole and said, "Well, what do you think?"

"That dress is gorgeous; can I feel it? It looks so comfortable, and it's wrapped around you like a glove. You look amazing!"

"Thanks! I've never owned real cashmere before." She walked over to Nicole. "Here, feel it! Rub your face on it."

Nicole rubbed her cheek against the fabric. "Oh my gosh, it's so soft, like so much softer than regular wool."

"Right? What do you think about the boots?"

"They are both fabulous. I'd probably fall and break an ankle if I tried to walk with the stiletto heels, but you've aways been able to walk in gravity defying shoes."

"Nicole, you are doing a fine job stomping around in those moon boots. You could manage these." Zaina flexed her ankle.

Nicole started laughing and Zaina joined her and then they were both laughing so hard they couldn't breathe.

"Oh no, now my makeup is running," Zaina gasped.

"H-here is a t-tissue."

"Thanks." Zaina took the tissue and wiped her eyes. She unzipped her shoes and took them off, leaning back on the couch.

Nicole reached over and touched the swoop of hair across Zaina's forehead. "I love this look on you. With your delicate features, you can get away with almost any hairstyle, but this one is a sexy, glamorous, old Hollywood look. My only concern is the part where Jasper sees you and his eyes fall out of his head."

"Maybe I shouldn't wear my hair like this then."

"Z, don't turn down your beauty to make him comfortable!"

Zaina reached over and hugged her friend. "Thank you for saying that. I needed to hear it. When it comes to men, even in a fake dating scenario, I'm too quick to censor myself! I don't know why I do it!"

Nicole pulled back. "Will you promise me something?"

"Um, yes, sure."

"Promise me you'll be your big dramatic self from here on out. Stop shrinking to try to fit someone else's idea of you."

Zaina felt the sting of tears in her eyes. Her throat tightened and she couldn't speak for a moment. "Yes," she whispered, and then louder, "Yes, doggone it! You are right, Nic! I'm not shrinking for anyone! I can't believe I was starting to fall into an old bad habit! And Jasper and I aren't really dating! If there was any time I should be my loudest self, it's now!" Zaina shook her head, "Holy smokes, I didn't know how much I needed to hear that." She reached over and hugged Nicole again. "Thank you so much for your help."

Nicole patted Zaina's back. "That's what friends are for!"

They talked for a while longer, and then Nicole headed home. Zaina put their glasses in the sink and hung up her dress, and put the stiletto heeled boots back in her closet. She took a shower and then got under her covers.

Just as she was falling asleep, her phone chimed.

JASPER: Ready for tomorrow night?

ZAINA: (thumbs up emoji)

JASPER: Sweet dreams.

ZAINA: You too.

Chapter Twelve

♥

JASPER

Jasper rarely had on the TV when he got up in the morning, but ever since his appearance on Feel-Good Friday, he'd started putting on the Channel Twelve morning show. He had to admit; it wasn't a bad way to start the day. He'd forgotten the connection local television provided. This morning, Suzy Snow was warning everyone to stay home tonight. Up north, they were calling for white out conditions and down here by Marley Creek, it was looking like an ice storm was imminent.

"Suzy, the last two times the predicted winter storm missed us. As a matter of fact, last time I skipped my Pilates class, and we only got one inch of snow," Chrissy White said.

"I'm with Chrissy on this one, Suzy," Jasper said to his TV. Jasper shook his head. *I'm officially entering old age. Here I am sipping coffee and talking back to the people on the TV.*

"We've gotten lucky in the past, but today our time has run out. Everyone, please take precautions and stay in tonight!" Suzy Snow responded.

Zaina didn't know it, but Jasper was planning a surprise for their date tonight. He was picking up their dinner from Sean at five and then he was closing the taproom by six. They'd have the whole place to themselves. He knew Zaina was expecting their date to happen while the brewery was open, but he'd always planned to close early just this once, so they could have their date in peace. Plus, if they wanted to make social media content, they usually had to film it more than once to get the best result, and they certainly couldn't do that with his nosy regulars around. Now, with the potential for bad weather, no one, including Zaina, would think it was unusual for the taproom to be closed early. He hopped up and headed to the shower. He had a big day ahead of him and he wanted to make sure everything was perfect.

He was at Hop's Heaven by ten a.m. and spent the morning in his brewhouse checking on each of the beers that were currently fermenting. He was really looking forward to this year's Valentine's Day stout, Dark Chocolate Cupid. His goal was for it to come in with a nice seven percent alcohol content and a strong, but smooth chocolate flavor. He hoped Zaina would like what he came up with. He paused and did the math. Yes, their arrangement would last through Valentine's Day.

The workday went by quickly because all afternoon, they'd had a steady stream of people at the walk-up window stocking up with growlers or crowlers for the weekend winter storm. By four-thirty, it had started raining but the temperature was still too high for any ice and Jasper hoped that would continue.

"Jax, I'm heading over to Sean's place."

Jax was in the middle of closing out a tab and so they nodded in Jasper's direction and kept their focus on the customer. The rain was coming down harder now as Jasper drove over to Sean's. He parked and ran inside Jesse's Pub.

Jasper walked over to the bar where carryout orders were picked up and waited for help. The chalkboard at the bar said today's special was half-price appetizers from three p.m. to six p.m. Only four of the tables were occupied with customers.

"Hey buddy," Jasper said as Sean came out of the kitchen.

Sean gave Jasper a hug, "Hey man, crazy day huh? It's usually packed for half-off happy hour, but everyone seems to be hunkering down at home for whatever is going to happen. Is the big date still a go?"

"Yep. As soon as I get back with this food, we're closing for the night and Zaina will come over by six-thirty."

"Fantastic. This bag here is the surf and turf. Then I put in a baguette with the honey butter and a couple of spring greens salads with our homemade house dressing. For sides, I checked with Nicole, and she said Zaina doesn't really like broccoli so I did some sautéed haricot verts and of course, you can't go wrong with our mashed potatoes."

"Thanks again, Sean. This is great!"

Sean held up a finger. "And in this bag, there is a tablecloth, candles, and two of our best place settings. You may be in a brewery, but your dinner table is going to be five-star."

Jasper grinned widely and took the bags from Sean. "I don't know what to say, Sean! You're the best!"

"Have a great night and just bring back my stuff next week."

"You got it, bud! Have a good one!"

Jasper carefully loaded his car and drove back to the brewery. He only passed a couple of cars on his way back to Hop's Heaven and found only a few cars in the parking lot, aside from Jax.

He brought everything into the brewery and put it on the bar. "Jax, you can leave. I'll close everything out."

"Are you sure Jasper?"

"Yes, thanks for all your help today. Be careful driving home. I know you have a long drive."

"I'll see you Sunday!" Jax put on their bomber jacket and pulled a cap over their long brown hair and walked to the door.

He turned to the rest of the taproom. "Jax did last round already, right?" A couple of construction workers at the bar nodded and finished their beer.

"If you don't mind, I'm going remote start my car and finish this scene." Kathy said.

"If there is one thing I know, it's don't mess with Ms. Kathy when she is in her writer flow."

"I've taught you well, Jasper." Kathy said nodding.

The two construction workers left the bar, giving Jasper a wave and a nod. Jasper checked his phone, no texts from Zaina and it was six p.m. He taped a *Closed for a Private Event* sign on door. Then he turned down the bar lights and picked up the tableware that Sean had given him and walked over to the table that was his favorite to sit at when he was in the taproom. He took out the black tablecloth and spread it out.

Kathy closed her laptop. She took her reading glasses off and hung them on her flannel shirt. She walked over to Jasper. "Here, let me help you set the table."

"You don't have to do that Kathy; you should get home to your family."

"It's just me and my cat and no cat lady jokes, please! I only have one cat!"

"Do I ever make fun of you, Kathy?"

Kathy put her hands on her hips, "Of course! It's what we do!"

Jasper's eyes twinkled. "You got me there! Here's the silverware."

"Too bad you don't have any flowers."

"I should have thought of that, but it's too late now. Luckily, Sean gave me candles."

"Dinner by candlelight with a handsome man that is interested in her. Zaina is going to love this! I need to let you in on a secret about women. We love when a man is interested enough in us to make an effort. We don't expect perfection or the perfect date, we just want a good man who wants to know us better and will show themselves in return."

Jasper took out the candle lighter and lit the two taper candles. Jasper and Kathy admired the table.

"As a romance professional, I can confirm that this table looks full of romantic potential. And I know Sean's food always hits the mark. Now all you need to do is open up to the possibilities of where things could go with Zaina, and this might be the best date of your life."

Jasper was stunned silent, a rare state for him.

"Just think about it," Kathy implored.

"I will," Jasper promised.

Kathy went back to the bar and got her tote bag.

"Kathy, do you need some help outside?"

She waved him off. "I'll be fine."

"I'm going to walk you out, just to be safe."

"Alright." She walked out the door, and Jasper followed on her heels. The wind was picking up, but the precipitation was still liquid. Kathy got in her car and honked as she left the parking lot. Jasper rushed back inside. He checked his phone again and went into his office to find a playlist on his computer to play over the brewery sound system.

Once that was squared away, he took out the dress shirt he'd brought to work for their date. It was a solid lavender button down. He took off his flannel shirt and the Hop's Heaven logo shirt he was wearing underneath, then he put on his dress shirt. He undid the first couple buttons since he wouldn't be wearing a tie and he changed out of his work boots and jeans and put on a pair of slim-cut chinos and a pair of black dress sneakers.

He checked his look in the mirror on the back of his office door. Jasper had given himself a close shave this morning, and even though it was past five o'clock, he didn't have a five a clock shadow. When he was a teenager, he'd been bummed at his inability to grow a decent mustache and the lack of hair on his chest, but over time he'd learned, among other things, plenty of women appreciated his bare chest and not having a stubble burn.

The headlights of a car flashed through the window of the brewery. His stomach filled with butterflies and his hands started sweating. The chirp-chirp of a car lock sounded, and he shook out his arms and tried to look casual. *Should I go open the door for her?* He rushed over to the door, just as she was opening it, and suddenly, she was there in the vestibule, inches from his chest.

"Well, hello there." Zaina looked up and batted her eyes at him.

"Hi." He said. He reached out and smoothed the swoop of blonde hair that was getting in her eyes.

"I like the new hairstyle."

"Thank you," Zaina said, and she fiddled with a dangling sliver filigree earring she was wearing. "Are you going to invite me in? I didn't think the brewery was going to be closed."

"I thought it would be more comfortable for us." He took her hand and led her into the taproom and over to the table. He pulled out a chair, and she sat down.

"Thank you."

"Should we do the social media content first?" Jasper asked.

"Let's do a selfie and post that right away."

Jasper sat down next to Zaina, and he held up his phone. His heart was beating faster, and as she leaned into him, he breathed in her scent. She smelled spicy, like cardamon and pepper. He wanted nothing more than to kiss the spot right below her ear. He put the arm not holding the cellphone around her shoulders and she cuddled into him. He felt like he was on a ladder and if he didn't hold perfectly still, he'd fall into the abyss, which would be fine if she were there.

"What if we look at each other instead of at the camera?" Zaina suggested.

"Okay," Jasper said, his voice deepened. They turned and looked at each other and he felt a pull he could not ignore. He looked down at her full, lush lips the color of wine and then his eyes flicked up to hers. Her pupils were wide, crowding out the deep brown of her irises. He tilted her chin up with his finger. He could see she was breathing harder now.

"Can I?"

"Do it," she whispered and when he was millimeters away from her lips, he stopped.

"Did you mean take the picture or kiss you?"

"Both," she said breathlessly. He dropped the phone and pulled her to him.

"Social media content later," he said and smashed his lips against hers. She let out a tiny moan, and he felt it in his groin. He wanted her, more than he'd wanted anyone or anything. He bit gently on her bottom lip and kissed her again. She brushed her tongue against the seam of his lips, and he opened his mouth, welcoming her tongue. He couldn't get enough of her and he almost hyperventilated before she broke off the kiss. Jasper pressed his forehead to hers and they looked at each other. Her eyes were sparkling. "My face is covered with dark red lipstick, isn't it?"

She nodded and giggled. Zaina took her cloth napkin and began rubbing the makeup off his face. "When you suggested we met here for our date instead of going to an actual restaurant, I thought that was pretty lame, but now I'm glad we are alone."

He stared at her with a crooked smile. "I'm glad you came around."

Zaina finished fixing his face, and she tossed the napkin back on the table.

"What are we doing here, Jasper?"

"We can do whatever you want, Zaina."

"That's the problem. I don't know what I want."

"How about we enjoy the meal I had Sean prepare for us and then we can talk, or not, whatever you decide."

Zaina got up, smoothing her dress, "I'm going to go wash my hands. I'll be right back."

Jasper's heart dropped. He'd hoped after dinner they could hang out and talk like this was an actual date. But he'd forgotten none of this was real for Zaina. He felt a pang of hurt in his chest, but he didn't have anyone but himself to blame.

Chapter Thirteen

♥

ZAINA

Zaina washed her hands and then stared at herself in the mirror. She gently touched her swollen lips. That wasn't a simple staged kiss. She'd felt like she was on fire, and the only thing that could help was Jasper's soft lips against hers. When he'd nibbled on her bottom lip, she'd almost climbed in his lap to beg for more. What was happening to her? Why him, of all the guys in Marley Creek, why was Jasper Kane the one that had her panties soaking wet?

"What have you gotten yourself into?" she said out loud.

She needed to remember what this was all about, getting the money she needed to have a baby. And besides, Jasper wasn't into her. He was caught up in their moment. That's what this was about, they were just getting a little too into their characters. The Jasper she was kissing wasn't the real Jasper, it was the Jasper that was into her, a character in their play.

Her cheeks were still on fire, so she put water on a paper towel and patted her face. She straightened her dress and her stomach growled. Maybe Jasper was right. They should just enjoy the meal Sean had made for them.

The soft lighting of the candles cast shadows over Jasper's face that only increased his devastating beauty. He looked haunted as he sat at the table; he glanced up as she walked over and sat down. She turned and smiled at him. "What did you order for us?"

Jasper got up and brought two plated meals covered with silver cloches over to the table. He set one down in front of Zaina and the other in front of himself. Already on the table was a breadbasket covered with a napkin, and each of them had a mixed green salad topped with toasted walnuts and bleu cheese.

"Ready for the big reveal?" Jasper had his fingers on the knob of the cloche.

"Should we take pictures?" Zaina asked, her hand on her plate.

Jasper paused. He let go of the cloche, "I got it. We can take some pictures of you feeding me and me feeding you and we'll do the thing where we wrap our arms together and drink at the same time"

Zaina nodded, "Yes, that sounds great." She was feeling more relaxed now that they were back on their pseudo-business footing. Her stomach had calmed down, and she was ready to eat. "Do you have the stand for your phone?"

"I'll go grab it." Jasper got up and jogged back to his office and then back over to the table.

"Set the phone up, hit video, and we'll take our covers off at the same time," Zaina directed Jasper.

"Great idea, and let's do a toast. What should we toast to?" Jasper asked.

"Getting back up after you fall?" Zaina suggested.

"Perfect! Are you ready?"

"Yep." Zaina nodded.

"One, two, three." They lifted the covers off their dinners and made noises of praise. Jasper turned to the camera. "Thanks for coming along on our first date." He raised his glass and so did Zaina.

He nodded, and she said, "Here's to getting back up after you fall." They clinked their glasses and took a sip, then they put down them down and Jasper cupped Zaina's cheek. She looked at him and nodded slightly. He leaned into her and lightly kissed her lips, then he moved away and stopped the video.

"That was great! We can edit it later and I'll post it. If it's okay with you, I think that's enough social media for today." Jasper said.

"Let's go ahead and eat. I should head home early; in case the roads get bad."

Jasper picked up the breadbasket and took off the napkin and began unwrapping the sliced French baguette. Next, he took out a tiny ramekin wrapped in plastic wrap.

"Is that Jesse's Pub's signature honey butter?"

Jasper smiled widely. "Yep!" he said popping his p.

Zaina slathered the French bread with honey butter and took a bite. "I think I've died and gone to heaven."

"Wait until you try the steak. Sean marinades it in a Hop's Heaven stout."

"Listen, I've never had anything from Jesse's Pub that wasn't delicious."

Jasper and Zaina tucked into their meals for a time. They enjoyed the food and shared laughs at their best friends' Sean and Nicole's expense in the way only staunch friends can.

"Here, let me help you clean up." Zaina stood up and started collecting the debris on the table.

"I can pack up some of the leftovers for you to take home."

Zaina reached over and rubbed Jasper's arm. "That's so sweet of you. I'd love the rest of the steak, and any honey butter, and the bread."

"Your wish is my command." Jasper started packaging up Zaina's to go. She watched his face as he worked, enjoying the way he worried his bottom lip as he crimped the container shut. The twinkly light around the bar windows flickered and Zaina thought it was a trick of her eyes, but then the outside lights went dark.

"Crap, I think the power is out." Jasper said.

He picked up a candle and set it on the bar. "I'm going to get a flashlight. Just stay here for a second."

Zaina pulled on her coat.

The beam of a flashlight bounced around as Jasper returned. "Are you cold?"

"No, but I better get going. We can go over the video tomorrow or I trust you to make me look good. You can edit it and post it without my review."

"Thanks, Zaina. Thanks for coming out and having dinner with me."

"It is part of our deal, but yes, it was nice. I mean, I had a pleasant time."

Zaina pushed on the door handle, but nothing happened. She pushed again, and still nothing. Jasper pushed on the door, harder now, and it opened. The wind took it and it banged so hard against the building Zaina was afraid the glass would shatter. Jasper stepped out onto the pavement. He lost his footing and fell on his back. Zaina rushed over to him, only to slip on the black ice covering the parking lot and landing on top of Jasper.

"In other circumstances, this could be fun," He quipped. The wind took his words away before she could even be sure of what he said. She carefully got off Jasper. Shards of ice were pelting both of them as they struggled to stand up and make their way back into the vestibule of the brewery. The street and buildings around Hop's Heaven were completely dark. Zaina and Jasper worked together to pull shut the door amid the ice and the wind. They stared at each other. "Zaina, I can't let you drive home in this."

Zaina shook her head. "I don't want to drive home in this."

Crack! They turned toward the noise. A large tree limb was down in the street.

"Good gravy!" said Zaina.

"Well, that seals it. We're staying the night in my office. Good thing I still have a few throws and pillows with the Hop's Heaven logo that didn't sell at the live last week."

Jasper turned on the flashlight and started walking to his office. Zaina followed. Even amid a crisis, she couldn't help admiring how Jasper's ass looked in his chinos. He still had the same walk he'd had in high school. He walked on the balls of his feet instead of heel to toe. She'd had no clue why his twinkle toes walk got her heart racing, but she'd always loved it.

A splash of icy dread stopped the warmth that was pooling in her groin. She was stuck here with Jasper. How was she going to spend the night here? "Jasper," she said in a panic, "maybe I should go? This is too much."

Jasper opened the closet in his office and pulled out a couple of brand new blanket. He threw one to Zaina, who caught it and opened it. Jasper tossed the other one on his couch and then rummaged around in the closet, pulling out pillows with the Hop's Heaven logo.

"Zaina, you could fall and get a concussion just trying to get to your car. Then you'd have to chisel off enough ice to get in your car, and if you got out of the parking lot, you'd have to drive around that branch in the road. And who knows how many more branches are on the ground? Plus, what if you don't have power at home? At least here, we will have power for heat and the plumbing once the generator kicks in."

Zaina played absently with her earring. "I know you're right, but..." she trailed off, realizing she couldn't say: *I'm afraid I might accidentally sleep with you if I stay here, and I don't know if I can trust you.* She looked down at her outfit. Thank goodness the fall hadn't snagged her dress. It was a good thing she'd worn her Dr. Martens. If she'd had on her stilettos, she probably be praying an ambulance could make it her to take her to the hospital with a broken ankle.

Jasper was still in the closet. "Give me one sec, Zaina. I'm trying to find something for you. Ah-ha! I found it!" He turned around and handed her a double extra-large Hop's Heaven sweatshirt.

"Thank you?"

"It's the closest to pajamas I can offer."

"Oh my gosh! Thanks, Jasper. That's really sweet. You're right, I don't want to sleep in this dress." Zaina looked down at her feet, still clad in her boots. "You wouldn't have fuzzy socks, would you?"

Jasper grinned from ear to ear. "It's your lucky day."

He went back into his closet and came out with a pair of fuzzy black logo socks. "Here you go."

She shook her head. "You are all about the marketing."

"You know it. Someday, if I ever get married, I'm going to do that right here too."

"I don't have any doubt. You said we'll have heat even though the power is out? "

"Yes, I have a generator. It will kick in if the power is out for more than an hour, and that will keep the brewing safe. Plus, it will keep the heat on and we can use the bathrooms but it's not enough for the TVs or lighting, etc."

"That's great news. I'm going to go change."

"Do you need anything else?"

Zaina looked down. "No, I'm good."

Jasper handed her his flashlight, and she went to the bathroom to change. Zaina took off her dress and carefully folded it. She took off her bra and pulled the giant sweatshirt over her head. She folded the sleeves once, and then again, and then one more time. The sweatshirt came down to her knees. She put her bra inside her dress and carried everything back to Jasper's office.

When she walked into the office, Jasper had changed into a pair of sweatpants and a long-sleeved Hop's Heaven T-shirt. He was making a bed out of his couch.

"The couch is a futon, huh?"

"Yeah, when I was just starting this place, there were nights when I'd stay over just to make sure everything was going okay with the beers." He looked sheepish. "I was pretty nervous. This place had to be a success. Look, I even found a sheet in the closet. It's clean!"

Zaina took off her boots and sat on the futon to put on her fuzzy socks. "I believe you. If you say it's clean and you only have a bed in your office because you are dedicated to your craft, whatever you say Jasp." She popped her p and winked. Jasper stopped scowling, realizing she was just messing with him. His face softened. She crossed her legs and sat back on the futon. She patted the space next to her. "Come sit down. It's been a long day."

"Who could have predicted this?" he said.

"I'm pretty sure Suzy Snow did." They looked at each other and laughed until tears were streaming down Jasper's face and Zaina was holding her side. "Ack, I have a side cramp. Stop making me laugh."

Jasper walked out of his office and came back with a couple of glasses of water. He handed one to Zaina. She took a long drink of water and steeled herself to ask Jasper the question she'd been waiting twenty years to have answered. "Jasper, why did you ghost me in high school?"

Jasper's face fell. She could see pain in his eyes, and she was tempted to tell him to forget it, that it had been a very long time and it didn't matter anymore. That would be a lie. It did matter to her, and she needed to know. She needed closure, and once she had that, she could stop ignoring the feelings popping up. She kept quiet and waited for him to speak.

He cleared his throat and took another drink of water, then he got up and put his empty glass on his desk. He sat back down next to her.

"I was a dumb kid. I liked you so much, Zaina. For months before the party, every day I would wait by my locker to glimpse you coming out of your gym class. You were always smiling and laughing with girls from your class. You didn't have a care in the world, and I just wanted to be near you. When you walked into that party, I had to talk to you. Everything I did and said that night was true. It was me. I wanted to go out with you the next Friday. I planned to call you the next day. I was going to wait for you to get out of gym so I could walk you to your next class. I was glad we didn't go further that night. I didn't want to have sex with you. I wasn't mad because you didn't want me to reach under your shirt." He pleaded.

Zaina cut in. "Why didn't you meet me after gym? Why didn't you stop the rumors that we'd had sex?"

Jasper frowned. "I was a coward. I wasn't strong enough to tell my friends that you were beautiful and the best kisser I would ever know and that nothing more happened. I was too desperate for friends and my parents' approval. I don't know how my mom found out about us at the party, but she did. The next day, she called me into the kitchen and told me if I wanted their support, if I wanted a car to drive and someone to pay for college, I needed to date people her and my father approved of, not some girl who dyed her hair black and who didn't even know who her father was." He spat out the last sentence as if the words tasted like castor oil.

Zaina let out a sob. Now she knew. It was just as awful and typical and mundane as it could be. How many times had a scenario like this played out in towns around the world. She felt the weight of not knowing and being afraid to just ask slide off of her. "You should have told me this a long time ago."

Jasper hung his head. "I should have, but I was too embarrassed. You deserve so much better."

"I know I do." Zaina said, her chin held high. "The thing is, it's all so boring."

Jasper raised an eyebrow. "Boring?"

"All this time, the big heartbreak of my high school days was the same old stuff you see in every teen drama. How boring it is that we dealt with this in real life? How boring that you couldn't stand up for me?"

Jasper nodded. "You're right, and I deserve your disdain. If it makes you feel better, every time I saw you, I was reminded of my failings."

"That just makes me sad for both of us."

Jasper sighed and ran his hands through his hair.

"I think," Zaina continued. "I think we've spent enough time in the past. Don't get me wrong, it was very important for us to have this conversation. Now we have talked and I'm ready to move on. Dwelling in the past has been doing me no favors for a very long time. How do you feel?"

"The knots in my stomach are gone. I'm sorry. I should have told you a long time ago."

Zaina put her hand on Jasper's chest. She could feel his heart beating through his shirt, and it slowed as she spoke. "You've apologized, I've accepted your apology, now we get to have good things." She leaned in and gently brushed her lips over his. He gasped in surprise. She startled and moved back, but he pulled her to him and then his lips, those soft full lips that made her ache just to see them, were on hers and he was nibbling on her bottom lip, and she was wrapped in his arms.

She breathed in the citrus scent of him and pushed her tongue into his mouth. She needed the taste of him. Especially now that the air had been cleared. She wanted him on top of her. She longed to have him pressing her down, gripping her thighs and burying himself in her. She moaned, unsure if it was her thoughts getting her wet or the way his tongue was exploring her mouth. He pulled back, gasping, and looked at her.

"You're so fucking hot, Z."

Zaina was feeling bold and reckless, so she took his hand and pressed it to the v of her legs so he could feel what he did to her. "This is what you do to me, Jasper," she said. He used his thumb to trace the outline of her panties, and then he ran his thumb over her clit through the thin fabric. "Lie back," he told her.

She laid down on the futon, propped up on her elbows. He reached under her sweatshirt and rolled her tights down to her hips. She lifted her hips, and he grabbed on to her ass. She felt the scrap of his calluses against her bottom and then her tights were gone.

"Zaina, I have been wanting to know how sweet your pussy is for so long now. I know it's going to taste sweeter than any beer I've ever made."

Zaina batted her eyes at Jasper. She was enjoying finally doing what she wanted to do with her life. "Jasper, I want your head between my legs. I want you to lap up my pussy juices like ah…"

"Like it's the foam on the top of a freshly-poured barrel aged stout?"

"Yes," Zaina nodded. "Just like that."

"Your wish is my command." He moved down between her legs. She reached down and ran her hand through his hair, and then she gently pulled it. He groaned and used his tongue to push her thong to the side, he put his mouth on her nub. Jasper began sucking on her, and she started rocking her hips. He squeezed her ass and tilted her up. He took a finger and slid it into her wet juices and then pushed it into her, slowly drawing it in and out as his tongue circled her clit.

She whispered, "Right there. Oh yes, give me more."

"Do you want another finger, Z?"

"Yes, give me more."

He pushed another finger into her. She was getting close now. She ground into him as he sucked on her swollen bud. "Come for me," he cheered her on. She rocked against him harder now. Her hand was tight in his hair, and balance on the edge of climax.

"I can't, I can't," she said. Then he gently squeezed her clit, and it pushed her over the precipice. She shuttered as her orgasm tore through her.

"God, you are so beautiful when you are coming."

She pulled Jasper up to her and kissed herself off his face. She held his cheek in her hand. "You're so beautiful when you are eating me out."

Chapter Fourteen

♥

JASPER

Jasper had never been this hard in his life. "Zaina," he said, but she interrupted him with a hand down his sweatpants.

She gasped, "You're not wearing underwear." Jasper kissed the delicate skin just under her ear. He'd been daydreaming about kissing her right there, and now he was. She slowly moved her hand up and down his cock. "I didn't realize how big you were. I don't even know if you'll fit." She said slyly, and then she pushed him back on the futon. She straddled him, his sweatpants the only barrier between them. Zaina ground into him, and he put his hands on her hips. He began guiding her back and forth along his shaft. The fabric of his pants only intensifying his desire to be inside of her.

She paused and he whimpered. She moved off him and he sat up, looking at her confused. His balls ached with need. He took his cock in his hand and began slowing stroking.

"Let me help you," she said, and her eyes sparkled with mischief.

He moved his hand, and she hooked a finger into the top of his sweatpants and pulled them down, freeing him. "Why hello there," she said and then she took him in her mouth. She licked the vein on his cock and he started moaning. He didn't know how long he could hold on with her sweet lips wrapped around him. She cupped her hand on his balls, lightly fondling them as she sucked. He watched her work and his breath quickened with each lick of her tongue. Then she started humming "Eye of the Tiger" and he almost came. "Zaina, you're killing me. Oh, my god your tongue. Don't stop." He was thrusting into her mouth faster and his orgasm was just about to—then she stopped. He looked at her, panicked for a brief second that this was all a dream somehow.

She curled up against him. Throwing her leg over him she said, "Jasper, tell me you have a condom or three."

"Oh, fuck! Yes, of course!"

"Of course?"

"You would be surprised how often I have someone asking where the closest drug store is, so I started keeping a box on hand. It seemed less tacky than putting up a condom machine in the bathrooms. Hang on." Zaina moved her leg off him and Jasper hopped up and pulled open the bottom drawer of his desk. He took out a couple condoms. "Better to be safe than sorry."

He sat back down next to her on the futon. "May I take off your sweatshirt?" She raised her hands, and he pulled off the giant top. His jaw dropped; her perfect teardrop breasts were there in all their glory. "You're not wearing a bra."

"Nope." She smiled. He bent down and took one of her pebbled nipples in his mouth. Jasper sucked on the nub, hard enough to sting just a little and then he popped his mouth off it and blew on it. He savored the shiver he felt run through her and he repeated licking and sucking her other breast. He moved up, kissing the hollow of her collarbones. She leaned back, clad only in her bright pink thong. "Take your shirt off," she ordered.

"Yes, ma'am." He looked her in the eyes and stood up. He reached behind him and pulled the shirt off over his head in one quick move. She looked up, admiring the bare skin of his chest and his washboard stomach. Zaina stood up and traced the light trail of hair that started at his belly button and moved down to his cock.

She caressed his obliques. "You are as gorgeous as I imagined." She slid her hands down the back of his sweatpants and cupped his ass. She rubbed against him. He couldn't take it a moment longer. His large hands spanned her waist, and he picked her up. She wrapped her legs around him, and Zaina kissed his neck. She sucked on the tender skin of his neck, just enough for him to feel it, but not enough to leave a mark and the feeling struck him like a lightning bolt straight to his shaft.

He turned and placed her on the futon. Jasper shucked off his sweatpants, taking out a condom. He opened the wrapper and slid the condom down over his throbbing cock.

Zaina lay back on the bed, her legs wide. Jasper watched for a moment as Zaina rubbed her hand over her swollen clit. She licked her lips. "I can't wait for your massive cock to fill me up."

He took his finger and slide it into her wet pussy. "You're so ready for me."

She moaned and squirmed as he added a second finger to his thrusting. He was as wound up as he could be. "I need to be in you now."

"Jasper, please." She begged.

He picked up a pillow and whispered in her ear, "lift your ass." He moved the pillow under her bottom. Then he took his cock and teased her entrance while his thumb circled her clit. He tortured both of them as he took his time slowly pushing himself into her pussy. Once he was deep inside her, he slowly pulled in and out. She was moaning now, and the urgency of her sounds hit him to the core, bringing him closer to his own orgasm.

He took one of her legs and put it over his shoulder allowing him to be even deeper in her and he began pumping in and out, her tight pussy the perfect size for his swollen cock. Zaina began yelling his name and that completely undid him. He came hard. They rocked together, both squeezing every aftershock from their orgasms.

He lay on top of her, kissing her neck and lightly rolling her nipple between his thumb and forefinger as they caught their breath. Jasper could listen to the beat of her heart every night for the rest of his life. The peace of being with her in the afterglow of their fantastic sex surprised and pleased him. He got up and took care of the condom then he put on his sweatpants and a pair of fuzzy socks. He handed Zaina her giant sweatshirt. "Can I get you something to drink? Do you need anything?"

She pulled the sweatshirt on and sat so that the sweatshirt was completely covering her legs. "Actually, I'm kind of hungry now. Should we eat the leftovers?"

"Does great sex always make you hungry?"

Zaina smoothed her hair in thought, "Yes, I do like an after-sex snack. Do you not?"

"If it's an after-sex snack with you, I'm all in." Jasper tossed his hair. "I'm going to go wash my hands and I'll get our food."

"I'm going to go to the bathroom, too. Can't be getting a UTI."

"Definitely not!"

Jasper set up their spread on his desk and waited for Zaina to return from the bathroom.

Zaina came back and made a beeline for the food. "Do you mind if I take the last of the bread?"

"No, of course not."

"Great," she said and slathered honey butter all over the last slice of bread. "This honey butter is so good; I want to save the rest of it and then later I'm going to put it on your cock and lick it off."

Jasper's cock stood at attention. "Zaina, you are full of surprises." They ate the remains of their dinner. Later, Zaina was in the mood for a very special midnight snack.

Chapter Fifteen

♥

ZAINA

Zaina and Jasper woke up when the overhead lights flickered back on at eight in the morning.

She wrapped a blanket around herself and tiptoed to the bathroom. As she was washing her hands, a smiling Zaina reflected back onto her. What a night. She'd actually licked honey butter off Jasper. And my goodness, what a spectacular cock that man had! The entire night had felt like a fever dream. She had trouble believing it had happened. She rinsed off her face and then padded back into Jasper's office.

The harsh light of day made the connection she'd felt with Jasper the night before fade. He'd gotten dressed and was lacing up his boots. "The power is back on; did you see if the road was clear?"

"No, I didn't notice." Part of Zaina had hoped they could crawl back under the patchwork of throws where they'd been spooning and forget the world for a little longer.

"I'll go check." He walked by her and gave her a pat on her head while he was staring at his phone.

Zaina didn't know what to make of his behavior. Last night had been mind-blowing, and that was before they'd had sex. She'd felt like a superhero last night, completely in control and able to forgive old slights. Today she was unsure of herself, and more unsure of his feelings. Last night, she'd looked in his eyes and saw longing and desire. Today, so far, all she'd seen was the reflection of his phone screen in those bottomless brown eyes. She sighed. Maybe what they'd had last night was a fantastic night that brought closure to the past and nothing more. If so, she could deal with that.

What she wanted most at this point in her life was to be a mom, and she didn't know if starting up a relationship with Jasper would be a good idea. She'd need to focus on taking care of herself and preparing for artificial insemination, and if all went well, being pregnant in the second half of this year.

Zaina walked over to Jasper's desk and found a charger for her phone. His laptop was opened and on the screen was a spreadsheet with a column of potential investors and then columns filled with dates. She noticed her stepfather's venture capital company was on the list as having been contacted. That was another reason it was okay that nothing else happened between them. Jasper's focus was on his business's success. She wasn't going to take second place to a man's job, especially if it was someone she was going to marry. She didn't need a husband. If she decided to get married, she would not marry someone whose career came first. Their family would always need to come first.

Zaina heard the ding of the front door, and a moment Jasper walked back into his office.

"Good news! The road is clear! I went outside to put some salt down and it's only drizzling, no more ice. In fact," he pulled out his phone, "the temperature is in the mid-thirties."

"That is good news! I could use a hot shower."

Jasper gave her a smile and raised his eyebrow. "Need anyone to scrub your back?" His eyes slowly flicked down her body.

She felt heat rise on her face. "Tempting as that thought is, I've got a ton of work to do today."

Jasper lowered his eyes and nodded. "Gotcha. Well, I'll get to work on a video clip from the footage that we shot."

"I'll trust you to put up something good. Just post whatever you decided. You don't have to send it to me first," Zaina said as she pulled on her tights under the giant sweatshirt. "Hey, I'll get this washed and bring it back over."

"No worries, Z. Sorry, I don't have any coffee on hand."

"I'm more of a tea drinker, and I've got all sorts of tea blends at home, so I'm set."

"Okay, well, then, whenever you're ready, I'll walk you out." Jasper stood leaning on the door jamb.

Zaina put on her boots and tied the laces. She made sure she had her purse and the bag with her dress and everything else. She stood up and walked to the doorway where Jasper was standing. He grabbed her free hand to hold it as they walked out. She loved the way his big hand swallowed hers whole. The roughness of his palm comforted her. She'd always loved feeling the calluses on a man's hand.

They didn't speak as they walked through the brewery. Too soon, they were standing at the front door. "Send me a text so I know you got home, okay?"

"Are you staying here?"

"I'll work on our video, and I have to send out a few emails and then I'll head home, too."

"Text me when you do so I know you got home okay."

Jasper snickered, "Yes ma'am. You take care." He bent down and kissed the tip of her nose. She turned and walked out. The rain was falling harder now, so she put up her hood and walked as quickly as possible to her car. She considered running, but the very last thing she wanted to do today was fall flat on her face in front of Jasper. Hopefully, after last night, she was done falling for the rest of the year.

The drive home was uneventful. The streets were almost empty, but at least all the precipitation had stopped. Zaina wanted to relax in a hot bath and then take a nice, long nap, but Saturday was usually her busiest day in the shop. She took a quick hot shower and tried not to think about whether Jasper was acting weird this morning. In short order, Zaina was in her shop, pouring herself a cup of tea.

Foot traffic was slow, and Jasper was never far from her thoughts. After a couple of hours, she texted her friends Nicole and Devin.

> Z: I need my girls.

NIC: What's up?

> Z: Me and Jasper.

DEV: You didn't?

> Z: All night long.

NIC: Damn Girl!

DEV: Mm-hmm, so how can we help?

Z: It got weird this morning. I need to talk it through.

DEV: Why don't you two come over tonight for pizza? Ben's out of town.

Z: Perfect. How about you, Nicole?

NIC: You sure you don't want me to have Sean whip some food up for us?

Z: Now that Devin said pizza, I've got a huge taste for Best Pizza Near Me.

NIC: Best Pizza Near Me it is! See y'all tonight!

The rest of the workday passed far too slowly for Zaina; she was driving herself up the wall by closing time. She drove over to Devin's house and pulled into the expansive driveway next to Nicole's car. She got out of her car as Nicole was getting out of hers.

Nicole walked over and gave Zaina a hug. "It's so good to see you," Nicole said.

Zaina giggled. "I saw you last week. You're so funny."

As they walked up the steps to Devin's door, she opened it.

"Come on in, girls. The pizza should be here in about fifteen minutes."

Zaina walked into Devin's house and stood in the foyer with Nicole as they unlaced their shoes and took them off.

"Give me your coats," Devin said. She hung them up in the coat closet, then they walked down the hall to her great room. Devin had wine, beer, and water set out to drink. Zaina poured herself a glass of white wine. "Nicole, do you want a glass, too?"

"Sure, Z," Nicole said as she pulled out a chair from the pub height table that overlooked the sunken living room. On the far wall was a fireplace with a TV mounted above the mantle. A kids' cartoon was playing, but the twins were nowhere to be found.

Zaina walked over to Nicole and handed her a glass of wine. "How about you, Devin? Red wine?"

"Yes please," Devin said. She turned off the children's show and put on music.

Devin sat down in a chair with a groan. Her hair was wrapped in a scarf, and she was in loungewear.

"Devin, you look exhausted. I feel bad that you're hosting tonight," Nicole said.

"Franklin and Liam have been giving me a run for my money lately."

"What's going on?" Zaina asked.

"I don't want to take over the conversation. We're here about you, not me."

Zaina put her hand over her friends. "We can talk about you first. Maybe we can help?"

Devin let out an enormous sigh. "I'm just so damn tired; we all are. Ben is out of town at least three days each week. I've got a law practice to run and all the mayoral duties, many of which could just be an email instead of a meeting, but I can't say that.

It's an election year. I need to be available for the people and the town council. Liam is having night terrors. He wakes up screaming between two and three a.m. every night."

Her eyes filled with tears. "It's so scary when he is going through it. He doesn't even recognize me and then, of course, it wakes up Franklin as well and he cries because he is afraid for his brother. Then I'm crying and I don't know what to do." Tears were streaming down Devin's face.

Nicole got up and started rubbing Devin's back. "You poor thing. How can we help?"

"I have no idea, I've been so tired for the last couple of weeks. Yesterday I wore two different shoes to court. To court!"

"That's not good," Zaina said and immediately bit her lip, wishing she could take it back.

Devin hit the table. "I know! I've got to get some sleep. If only I could make the night terrors stop, but there isn't much that can be done. All I can do is hope Liam will outgrow it and hope Franklin doesn't start having them."

"Devin, I know you're not keen on it, but maybe take this as a sign that it's time to get a nanny," Zaina suggested, and she poured a little more wine into Devin's glass.

"Ugh, I know you are right, but I don't know. I don't have the time and energy to find and interview a nanny. I know it sounds ridiculous, but I also don't want to have another woman in my house. It just rubs me the wrong way."

"It may seem ridiculous, but you are a Sagittarius." Zaina explained.

"What if," began Nicole, "I knew of someone who had years of experience babysitting children, plus a couple of years of college under their belt majoring in elementary education, and who is currently looking for a steady job?"

Devin rubbed her temples. "Tell me more about this person."

"Sean's stepbrother, Ethan. He's been in town for a few months now. He watched younger kids and worked at a day camp when he was in high school and then he was going to college for elementary education—"

"What happened there? Did he get kicked out? Drugs? Alcohol?" Devin questioned.

"It was a bad breakup. Depression set in and he withdrew before he failed all his classes. He went to live with his dad for a while, but Ethan and the wife don't get along. That's when Sean's dad asked if Ethan could come live here, and he's been staying at Sean's place and working for Jasper. He's a good guy, volunteers at the animal shelter and he's great with little kids." Nicole said.

"Can you and Sean vouch for him? And I'd run a background check, of course."

"For sure. I can give you Ethan's information if you'd like to call him and set up a time for him to come meet the boys."

"Yes, let's do that." Devin smiled. "I had this idea of a nanny as a tiny young girl coming into my house and disrupting it. It never crossed my mind that I could look into having a manny. The boys are such high energy kids; they really need someone who can keep up with them."

Nicole picked up her phone and sent Devin Ethan's contact info. "There you go."

Devin put on her glasses and picked up her phone. She unlocked it and sent a quick text to Ethan. "You're a lifesaver, Nicole!"

"I'm just glad I could offer a potential solution."

"Now that we've made strides with my issue, let's talk about you, Zaina. What happened with that tall, gorgeous man?"

Ding-Dong

"Pizza Pizza's here! I'll go get it!" Zaina hopped up and ran to the door. A few minutes later, everyone had a plate full of pizza and salad.

"Now where were we?" asked Nicole.

"Zaina was going to tell us all about her date with the super-hot Jasper." Devin replied.

Zaina blushed, but she didn't lower her eyes. "Girls, it was...a night to remember. When I'm old and gray in a rocking chair at the Marley Creek Retirement Village, and you see me smile wistfully, know I'm thinking about my night iced-in with Jasper."

"What happens next?" Nicole asked.

"Honestly, I don't have a clue. We didn't talk about anything. It wasn't like he asked me out or that I asked him out. When morning came and the very unflattering florescent lights came on in his office, it was like a switched turned off in each of us and we were almost back to where we started."

"Could it be all the sexual tension y'all had built up over your fake dating overflowed and this was just something you two needed to get out of your systems?"

Zaina nodded her head slowly, reflecting on Devin's words. "Maybe that's what it was. That could be it."

"So, it was just sex? You guys don't have any feelings for each other?" asked Nicole.

"I don't know. Maybe? It's too soon to say."

"Would you want to have a relationship with him?" asked Devin, who was always good at cutting to the chase.

Zaina swirled the wine left in her glass as she pondered her feelings. "Sometimes I think I would like to be with Jasper, but whenever I think about that, he'll start talking about his five-year plan to become the next national craft-brewery sensation, and then I remember who he is."

"And who is that?"

"Someone who puts business above love and family."

"Are you saying that if you thought he'd put you first, then you'd want to pursue a relationship with him?" Devin asked.

Zaina spoke in a whisper. "Yes." Then she was louder as she continued, "But that won't happen."

"Are you sure about that? That's not the vibe I get from him at all" Nicole said and finished her glass of wine.

"You don't believe me?" Zaina asked Nicole.

"No, it's not that I don't believe you. I guess I see something different when Jasper looks at you than you see."

"What's that?" Zaina had to ask.

"He'd do anything for you."

Zaina looked at her friends' faces. They were seeing something very different from what she was seeing. What if they were right and she was wrong? How could she know for sure Jasper would put her first and not his world domination plans? Did she care enough for him to try to figure out his intentions beyond what he might tell her?

"Zaina," said Devin, "What are you thinking?"

"It's pretty wild to me that you two apparently see a completely different Jasper than I do, and frankly, I don't know exactly what to make of it," Zaina blurted out.

"Don't you have a few weeks left of your fake relationship?" asked Nicole.

"I agreed to work with Jasper until March first."

Nicole twirled her wavy auburn hair as she thought for a moment.

"By the way, Nicole," said Devin, "I love that shirt on you. It shows off all your curves."

Nicole's cheeks reddened. "Thanks, Devin. Actually, Sean got it for me."

"Sean can cook, and he knows how to shop. Okay! When are you going to marry that man?"

Nicole rolled her eyes. "Don't rush us along, Devin, just because you are tired of being the only married one of our bunch."

"Nic, don't be rude. I just think he is the best thing that has ever happened to you," Devin explained.

"I'm sorry. I was being rude. Nancy and some of my other coworkers keep asking me when Sean is going to pop the question, and it's really getting old." Nicole frowned.

Devin reached over and held Nicole's hand. "Apology accepted."

"And you're not wrong," Nicole agreed. "Sean is the best. Now, back to Zaina and Jasper. Zaina if you are unsure of your feelings and you aren't sure you can trust Jasper yet, there is no hurry to figure anything out right now. Maybe if you two fake date enough, you'll figure out your real feelings."

Zaina got up and put her arm around each of her friends. "You two are truly the best. I don't know what I'd do without you."

"Luckily for you, you'll never have to find out." Devin assured her friend.

Chapter Sixteen

♥

JASPER

Jasper poured a pint of Lupercalia Lager for Sean and pushed it over to him. "I tapped the first keg of this today. Let me know what you think."

It was Monday around two p.m.; the brewery would soon fill up with the afternoon crowd of construction workers, but right now, there was just Sean and a few regulars sprinkled throughout the taproom. Since Jesse's Pub was closed on Mondays, Sean would often come over to Hop's Heaven to have lunch and a beer or two with Jasper.

Sean took a sip of the golden colored beer with the foamy head. He leaned his head from side to side and then he took a nice big gulp. He put down his glass and said, "I like it, refreshing, not to filling, nice and crisp. Not sure what's up with the name, though."

"Lupercalia was a pagan festival that happened on February fifteenth. As you know," Jasper drew a line across his chest where his shirt was embroidered with Hop's Heaven in gold thread, "I love alliteration. When I heard there was a pagan ritual that was the precursor for Valentine's Day, and it started with an L, I was almost required to brew a beer and call it Lupercalia Lager."

"What was the festival about?"

"Actually, it was pretty shady. It started with some animal sacrifices and then they moved on to whip women, all in the name of fertility."

"I can see why it's not celebrated anymore. Whipping ladies!?"

"Uh-huh," Jasper nodded.

"It's still a heck of a nice beer, Jasp."

Jasper clinked his five-ounce taster glass against Sean's pint. "Thanks, buddy."

"How's things with Zaina?"

"I'm kind of glad you asked."

Sean leaned in and took another swig of his of his drink. "Talk to me."

Jasper gave Sean an abridged version of his unforgettable night with Zaina.

"What's the problem?"

"I don't know, I just thought…"

"What, Jasper?"

"We had such an amazing night and the next day it was just back to business."

"Huh. Did you ask her out on a date or anything? How did things end that day?" Sean asked.

"I walked her to the door and asked her to text me when she got home, and she said she would."

"Did she?"

"Yes, she did."

"What happened after that?" Sean asked.

Jasper hung his head. "Nothing happened. I didn't know what to say, and she didn't text me again, so we haven't talked."

"And that's the problem."

"Yep. Sean, I really like Zaina. You know I've had a thing for her for ages, and finally we cleared the air about the past and we had the best sex I have ever had in my life, and then nothing."

Sean rubbed his chin in thought, "Well I'm sorry about that, Jasp. Maybe it's just not meant to be." He shrugged.

"Thanks, man. It's probably for the best. I'm getting some traction with my list of potential investors thanks to the viral clips and the appearance on Feel Good Friday. I need to stick with my plan and not get sidelined by lust or whatever I had with Zaina the other night."

"Yea, I think you're right, Jasp. Better to stick to your plan. How long are you and Zaina going to be doing your fake dating thing?"

"We're doing it through February."

"Okay, well maybe if there is something between you two, the next few weeks of your fake dating will bring it to the surface, and if not, well then you know that too," Sean suggested.

Jasper pulled his hair back in a ponytail and held it. He let out a breath, "Alright, that's what I'll do. I'm sure it's for the best. Zaina has never been a big fan of mine. I shouldn't expect that one night together could have changed everything between us."

Sean shook his head. "Sorry about that, buddy."

"No big deal. I've got a ton of work to focus on and I still get to spend time with Zaina."

Sean smiled slightly into his beer. It sounded like Jasper was really falling for Zaina. Hopefully, all this fake dating would lead

Zaina and Jasper to realize there was something between them worth fighting for, something like what he'd found with Nicole.

"I almost forgot. Ethan gave me his notice." Jasper said.

"He did?"

"Yep, last night. I told him I didn't need two weeks' notice and he could start his new job as soon as possible," explained Jasper.

"Ethan is going to be a great manny. He's always had a real knack with kids, like the kid whisperer."

"I'm sure it will be a better fit for him than working here." Jasper said.

"Thanks again for hiring him at all. I know you only did it as a favor to me."

Jasper cleaned glasses behind the bar as he listened to Sean. "No problem, that's what friends are for. I was happy to help, and it worked out perfectly. I had a few weeks of extra help at a low cost and now Ethan has found a job doing what he loves to do. I'll break even once we have no more broken glasses for a few months."

Sean chuckled, "Sorry, man."

"Like I said, no worries."

Jasper and Sean toasted and took a long drink of their respective beers.

"So, how are things going with your potential investors?" Sean asked.

"I've got a couple meetings scheduled later this month. They aren't at the top of my wish list, but if I can give a presentation, even if it's a no, that gets me one person closer to a yes."

"You'll get there, Jasper. I don't know of anyone else who has had such a solid vision for their business. Back when we met at that conference years ago, I knew when I heard you speak, you had the vision and passion to go far. We talked that evening, and I learned you had charisma as well. And the rest is really history."

"You really know how to gas a guy up. Thanks, Sean."

Jasper's phone pinged, and he pulled it out of his back pocket and swiped it open. The video clip he'd made from the ice storm date was posted and had over a hundred thousand views already. "Hey Sean, check your Instagram."

"Did you post a video?"

"Yes, we filmed it on Friday right before the ice storm hit."

Sean unlocked his phone and went to the Hop's Heaven account. He watched the reel that was quickly racking up thousands of views, then he put his phone away. "I can see why you have so many views."

"You can?"

"You two look like you're getting on like a house on fire. Seriously, the sexual tension in that clip is off the charts! Which is no surprise because…"

"Right, the best sex of my life happened right after. Maybe we just needed to get it out of our systems."

"Perhaps." Sean said. "Would you look at the time; I've gotta run. Nicole will be home from work soon!" He pulled on his coat and left.

Jasper turned his attention to reviewing the comments on his video. As he scrolled, one comment popped out at him. Mark Anderson had commented on the video. The comment said, "Looking good." Could that actually be the Mark Anderson of ADM investments? Jasper clicked on the comment and went to the profile. He hated to get his hopes up. It was probably one of the many spoof accounts on Instagram. However, this Mark

Anderson looked like it could be legitimate since he had only a few posts, and the posts that were there focused on Chicago sports. No controversial posts, and he had many more followers than people he followed.

Jasper wondered, *if this is the Mark Anderson, why is he posting on a Hop's Heaven video?* Maybe ADM investments was looking to add craft breweries to its portfolio. Jasper knew that ADM Investments had been bullish on the restaurant sector as of late and had invested in a new chain of Korean BBQ restaurants and a chain called Fakon and Eggs, a vegan breakfast chain. Jasper debated sending a direct message to the account. He wouldn't be surprised if the account didn't accept direct messages, but if it did, he had to try. If it was a scam account, at least he would know that as well.

Jasper crossed his fingers and clicked the message option, and it worked! He edited the email he'd crafted to reach out to potential investors since the appearance on Channel Twelve. Jasper double and triple checked the message for any typos and then he hit send. It was done now. Either nothing would happen or maybe he would get a reply. In the meantime, he'd better get back to work. There was a new beer to tap.

Chapter Seventeen

♥

ZAINA

Zaina was enjoying a quiet night at home. She'd spent her workday on her feet processing and packing orders to ship to new customers from not just the United States, but today she'd gotten her first order from Belgium. She'd gone upstairs and taken a nice, long hot bath. If the orders kept coming in like this, she was going to need to add a part-time person at the store. The arrangement with Jasper was really paying off. Not only was she going to be able to pay her large insurance deductible, the views from their videos and posts were bringing new customers to her store in droves. Thank goodness for the Internet.

She toweled off, moisturized everywhere, and put on her favorite flannel pajamas. She threw her clothes in the laundry basket and greeted her bed with a sigh. Sometimes there was nothing better than scrolling through social media in bed on a winter night.

After the first couple of videos Jasper had posted and tagged her in, she'd turned off her notifications because listening to all those pings, while good for her ego, was also draining her battery. Her phone buzzed with a text from Jasper. Her heart started beating faster despite her reservations about him. She could almost hear her mother telling her that actions speak louder than words. She clicked the text to read it.

JASPER: Holy crap! We knocked it out of the park this time! What should we do next?

ZAINA: What's going on?

JASPER: Have you not seen the video? Z, I put all my effort into making you look amazing and you don't even watch the final result? (pouting emoji)

ZAINA: My bad.

JASPER: No worries! You can watch it later. The point is, we've gotten more views on our date reel than we got for the original Frosty Toes video.That means people are following and sharing our content!

ZAINA: I've been slammed with online orders this week. I wonder how many people are going to my website. I never check the viewer stats.

JASPER: You should check! I'd love to know! I bet it's a hundred times what it was before.

ZAINA: That's wild!

JASPER: Just tell me I was right about this fake dating thing.

ZAINA: We haven't finished our contract yet. I don't want to jinx us. You know how social media can be.

JASPER: One day they love you, the next day they are doing take down videos about how you suck.

ZAINA: Exactly.

JASPER: Right now we need to make the most of this opportunity. What if you come here and we do a beer tasting?

ZAINA: Can I call you real quick?

JASPER: (thumbs up emoji)

Zaina punched in Jasper's number, and he answered on the first ring.

"Hey, you," he said in a voice that sounded deeper than she was used to. Then again, now that she thought about it, this was the first time she'd talked to him with her earbuds in. His voice went straight to her core. Again, her body wanted what her mind knew she should not have.

"Hi, Jasper." She said more breathlessly than she'd planned. "What's up, Z?"

She squirmed under her covers. "I thought it would be easier just to talk than to keep texting."

"I love hearing your voice, Z. Are you at home?"

A realization about where this phone call could go, if she let it, hit her and she wanted it to. Her pussy was wet now.

She whispered into the phone, "I'm in bed right now. It's been a long day."

She could hear a door shutting.

"And what are you doing in bed, love?"

"Talking to you?"

"Tell me more," he said, and she heard a zipper unzipping.

"I'm wearing my favorite silk pajamas."

"Short-shorts?

"Mm-hmm" Zaina said even though she was wearing flannel pajamas. She imagined herself wearing the silk pajamas she usually wore in the summer. She lifted her ass off the mattress and slid off her pajama bottoms.

"Z," he said, and Zaina imagined him in his office chair, licking his lips.

"I wish I was there with you right now. I'd climb into your lap and then I'd lean down and kiss your lips." She whispered.

"Zaina, my love, can you do something for me?"

Zaina logically knew she shouldn't like that Jasper had called her love, but right now, she didn't care.

"What's that, Jasp?"

"Can you touch yourself? Take those beautiful, manicured fingers and stroke that perfect little clit you have."

Zaina pushed her underwear to the side and began rubbing herself.

"Are you doing it, Z?"

"Yes, oh yes." She rolled her hips now. "Tell me about your cock, Jasper."

"It misses your sweet, pink lips on it." She heard a drawer slide open and the sound of a lotion bottle pump dispensing.

"Are you lubing up for me, Jasp?"

"Fuck me, Z," he said with a moan and then she could hear the sliding suck of his hand on his cock.

"If I was there, I'd put my lips on your cock, teasing the top of it until there was pre-cum and then I'll use my tongue to slide that pre-cum all the way down to the base. Next I'd move lower and put your balls in my mouth."

"Oh fuck, Zaina! How do you do that?" She could hear him moan low in his throat and she joined him, rubbing her swollen nub. They were both too close for talking now, the sounds of their breathing and lubricated fingers helping each of them climax.

Her legs were weak with aftershocks and her mind was blown. She was more than halfway through her thirties, and this was the first time she'd ever had phone sex, and to do it with Jasper, of all people.

Zaina curled up on her side as she listened to Jasper tidying up. "What was that?" she asked bemused.

"That was fantastic. You are so hot, Z."

Zaina giggled, "I might have a thing for your voice, Jasp. We may need to only text each other from here on out."

"By why, love? Why not enjoy each other, see where things go?"

"Oh Jasper, I don't want to be a downer right now, but you know we both have different goals."

"Zaina, you're right, I don't want you to be a downer right now. Let's talk about something else. What should we do for our next video?"

"Let me think…wait I've got it! What if you come to my shop and I'll do a tarot card reading. Maybe we can do it as a live?"

"If you're sure you want to it live, we can do that. I'm game for anything."

"Any-thing?" Zaina asked, dropping her voice an octave.

"Are you trying to start something? Do I need to come over there and give you a spanking?"

"Wouldn't you just love that?" she said.

"Yes, my love, I would." He ended the call.

Zaina flopped back on her bed, her face flushed and heat spreading low in her belly. How was she supposed to fall asleep now? She reached over to her bedside and pulled out her neon pink bullet vibrator. Once her need was slacked, she got up and went to the bathroom and got herself a glass of water. She came back to bed, tired and ready to call it a night, when she remembered she hadn't watched the video Jasper had texted her about in the first place.

She propped up her phone on her knees and clicked to watch. It was only a minute long. She finished it and immediately hit play again. She wasn't sure if she was really seeing what she thought she was seeing. Zaina shouldn't have been taken aback by the video. She had been there when they shot it. And the kiss they'd shared was seared in her mind.

It was still strange to see this version. The look in Jasper's eyes. He looked at her like she was a precious jewel that he was responsible for. He didn't look consumed with lust. He looked like a man falling in love. That couldn't be right. It must have been a trick of the lighting or the strangeness of the night. She'd felt like they were in an alternate universe during the ice storm, where their obligations and other needs were gone and all they needed to do was to be together.

She watched the video one more time. The best thing to do would be to just keep on doing what she'd been doing by keeping up her end of the fake dating bargain and not get hung up on Jasper, regardless of how everything about him made her wet. Zaina put her phone on the charger and finally went to bed. As she tried to fall asleep, the video and the soft look in Jasper's eyes as he watched her kept replaying in her mind.

Chapter Eighteen

♥

JASPER

Jasper hadn't stopped thinking about Zaina since their phone call the other day. If he was honest with himself, he hadn't been able to get Zaina out of his mind since she'd agreed to their fake dating arrangement. Today was the day she was going to do a live reading of tarot cards for him. He wasn't keen on the whole tarot cards stuff. Not that he believed in the cards, he definitely didn't. Jasper believed in forward momentum and the importance of having an unshakeable belief in himself, and what he didn't care for was anything that might make him question himself.

He closed his office door and walked over to the bar. "Jax, are you sure you don't need extra help tonight?"

Jax finished pouring a beer for Kathy and placed it in front of her. "I'll be fine, Jasper. Mondays are always slow."

"If you need me, just text me. I'll only be over at Zaina's shop."

"Hey, can you pick up my order while you're there?"

"You shop at Z's place?"

"She has the best tea blends in the suburbs."

"Good to know. Sure, I'll pick up your order and have it here for you tomorrow."

"Fab, thanks Jasper!"

Jasper gave Jax a wave and left for Zaina's shop.

He pulled into a parking spot in front of her shop. It was dark outside and he could see Zaina sitting in the yellow recliner. A cozy glow from an opulent chandelier above the table where Zaina was sitting made him think about what it would be like to walk through the door of his house and see Zaina sitting in his front room, waiting for him. He shook his head to push out the intrusive thoughts. She wasn't going to be his. Maybe he'd meet someone one day, but Zaina had already made up her mind about him and even though they'd been having some fun times, it wasn't anything real.

She had her life, and he was on track to, what? That's right, he was on track to having to have his brewery in towns across the United States. What could be better than that? He watched as Zaina stretched in her chair. She lifted her arms, and he could see the soft skin of her belly. She had a little freckle right by her belly button and he'd like to have his mouth on it right now. His pants tightened as he recalled the soft moans she'd made when they were on the phone together.

"Get a grip, Jasper!" he said aloud in his car. He turned off the engine and pulled out the key. Jasper got out of his car and clicked the lock button. He looked in the store window. Zaina had put down her cards and was walking over to the door.

"Howdy, stranger," she said, welcoming him into her shop. She held the door open as he walked in.

Jasper was unsure of himself. Should he give her a hug or a kiss on the cheek? Were they still in a business relationship or was it that plus more? He'd tasted every inch of her, but he wasn't sure if he was allowed to give her a quick kiss. He bit the inside of his cheek. Heat rose up his neck in his confusion. He unzipped his coat, and she stood watching, her hands behind her back. Jasper took off his coat and hung it up. He turned to Zaina, unable to stand his own awkwardness anymore, and he asked if he could give her a hug. "Can I," he began, but he felt so stupid, he changed course.

"Can you what?" Zaina asked as she rocked back on her heels.

"Get something to drink?" he finally finished.

"Of course! Do you want water or tea?"

"Water is fine. Also, I said I'd pick up Jax's order. I didn't know they came to your shop."

She handed him a water bottle, and he cracked it open.

"Jax is one of my regulars. In fact, that reminds me, I need to put a sex oil flyer in their bag."

Jasper choked on his water. "Sex oil?"

"Second only to success oil in my Etsy shop."

Jasper sat down in a chair. "I don't know how I feel about this."

Zaina was carefully spreading her red scarf on the table where she would do the live tarot card reading. She paused as she listened to Jasper sputter. "Jasper Kane, since when are you a prude?"

"Jax is barely 25!"

Zaina laughed, "Do you hear yourself, grandpa?"

Jasper ran a hand through his hair. "My God, you are right! When did I become a cranky old man?"

"Happens to the best of us! Does it make you feel better to know Jax is in a loving relationship?"

"Actually, that does make me feel better."

"Great, now are you ready to see what the cards have to say?"

Jasper fluffed his hair and straightened his shirt. "How do I look?"

"You are smoldering, and yet approachable." Zaina licked her lips slowly. "How about me?"

Jasper looked at Zaina appraisingly. Her long sleeve v neck shirt hugged her curves. He could just make out the points of her nipples through the thin material. He followed the line of her neck up to her cute little ears and he reached out and touched the long climber rhinestone earring in her right ear. Then he traced the line of her jaw with his forefinger, stopping when he got to her lips. "You're flawless."

She gave him a wink that went straight to his cock. One movement from her and he was straining his pants.

Zaina pulled out her Rider Waite tarot deck; it was the one she used for all her store readings. She began shuffling the cards. Jasper adjusted his phone on the stand they used to do their videos. "Are you ready for this to go live?" he asked.

Zaina gave a smile filled with bravado. "What do you have to lose?"

Jasper raised his eyebrow. "I think you are scaring me."

Zaina grinned wider and did an accordion shuffle. "Trust me."

Jasper nodded and counted down, "Three, two, one, and we are live at Zaina's shop New Age Stones and Witch Crafts! Hi, everyone! Tell us where you are watching from!"

Zaina continued to shuffle the cards, "And tell me what questions you want to ask the cards!"

They spent the next twenty minutes taking questions from the viewers watching the live stream and then Zaina said, "If everyone watching this live stream would like me to do a three-card tarot spread for Jasper, post a beer emoji in the comments." The screen flooded with beer emojis. Jasper mugged for the camera.

Zaina did some fancy card shuffles and said, "Jasper, the people want me to read your cards. Are you ready?"

"Anytime, Z!"

Zaina took a cleansing breath and then she took the deck of cards and moved them through the incense she had burning at her side. Next, she cut the deck into three, placed those face down on her red scarf and finally she reordered the cards into one deck, still facing down.

"Do you want to ask a specific question, or do you want a general reading?"

Jasper looked at Zaina and down at the cards. He wanted to ask what was going to happen at the end of their contract, but he didn't dare ask, not with over ten thousand people watching them. "Let's do a general reading."

"Outstanding!" Zaina took a slow breath in and out and pulled one card, then a second and third from the deck face down on her scarf. She paused for a moment before flipping over the first card. "This is the King of Pentacles." She lifted the card to show the viewers. "This card is all about material success, a life of luxury."

Jasper did a fist pump. "Fantastic!"

"Indeed. When this card shows up, it almost always means success in business." Zaina put the card down and said, "Are you ready for me to pull the next card?"

"I think I'm into this now! Bring on the next card."

Zaina pulled out a card that showed an angel pouring liquid between two chalices. It was facing Jasper instead of facing Zaina like the first card had been.

"Does that card mean that I make the beverage of the gods?"

Zaina laughed, her eyes lighting up in delight. "You're so silly. This is the Temperance card and the way it is shown means it's reversed."

"Oh no, temperance. Does that mean not drinking? Or since it's reversed, more drinking?" Jasper asked.

"You are all about the beer, aren't you?" Zaina quipped.

"I do make beer for a living!"

"True, but that's not what this card is about. When Temperence is reversed, it means you are ignoring something important to you, that you are close to giving up on yourself."

Jasper frowned. "Huh, that's good to know. I'm not sure what's it's referring to."

"Let's look at the last card and then maybe we'll have a better understanding of what the cards are trying to tell you."

Jasper rubbed his hands together. "Alright, what do I have to lose, right? Show me the last card!"

Zaina dragged the last card off the top of the deck and flipped it over. The card showed a man hanging upside down by one leg. His other leg was crossed and his hands were behind his head. Below the man's head was the title 'The Hanged Man.'

Jasper gulped visibly. "That can't be good."

Shocked face emojis flooded the comments.

"This card freaks people out the first time they see it, but if you know anything about tarot cards, you know that this doesn't mean something bad at all."

Jasper dramatically wiped his brow and said, "Phew, well, what does it mean, Z?"

"I like to say it means you are at a crossroads. You have a decision to make. Are you going to stay in the situation you are in? Or are you going to make a change? You are the only one who can decide if you move forward." Zaina explained.

"So let me get this straight," he tapped the King of Pentacles with his finger. "I'm on the road to riches."

"You could say that," Zaina affirmed.

"But I'm ignoring something that's important to me—which is clearly not beer," Jasper smiled and winked at the camera.

"You are so not ignoring beer!"

"And then we have the last card here," he put his finger on the hanged man card. "It seems like a terrible card, but it's not about being hanged, it's more about being hung up and stuck."

Zaina thrust out her hand. "Exactly! That's your three-card reading. What did you think?"

She peered into Jasper's eyes. He knew she was trying to read him, but he wasn't ready for that, so he looked at the camera. "Let's ask everyone watching what they think!"

"Alright, everyone, what do you think?"

Jasper and Zaina leaned in to see the screen.

"Veronica in Vermont thinks you should open a Hop's Heaven in her town," said Zaina.

"Veronica, I'd love to! If you know any investors, send them my way," said Jasper.

"Heather in Colorado wants to know if you do readings via Zoom, Zaina?"

"I do! Heather, go to my website for more details. Just search New Age Stones and Witch Crafts and I'll come up first."

"Tiffany in Southern Illinois wants to know when we are going to get married," said Jasper.

"Girl, slow your roll. We've only been dating a few weeks." said Zaina.

"Katherine in Indiana says we've been following you two since the Frosty Toes. #TeamZJ! ZJ, why am I second?" Jasper asked.

"Why not, Jasper, why not?" Zaina laughed.

"Y'all, thanks for tuning in tonight, but we gotta go!" Jasper put his arm around Zaina's waist and pulled her to him. She fell into his lap and knocked the camera over with her feet. Jasper picked up the phone and clicked off the video.

Zaina stayed in his lap for a beat longer and then she hopped up. "I think it went really well! What did you think?"

"I was worried about how the live would go, but that was perfect. Even knocking over the camera! I don't think we could have scripted anything better."

Zaina picked up her deck. She shuffled the deck twice, and then she put the cards back in their box.

"Boy, could you imagine if Veronica from Vermont actually knew someone who'd want to invest in a Hop's Heaven? Maybe that King of Pentacles was on to something."

Zaina frowned, "I suppose." She shrugged.

"Z, if our viral fake dating leads me to a franchise deal, I will not forget about how you made it happen. You have been doing such a great job helping us succeed and if, no, when I have the investors I need to franchise, I'll compensate you." Jasper spoke quickly, unable to contain his enthusiasm.

Zaina looked down and picked lint off her red scarf. "That sounds fine." She said blandly.

Jasper pursed his lips. She didn't sound excited about how well their viral marketing was working. "Would you not want a bonus?"

"If you want to give me more money for our fake dating contract, I'll take it." She walked over to the counter and put away the tarot cards and the scarf. "I can use the money and, like you said, I deserve it."

Jasper wanted to feel relieved, but he had an uneasy feeling that he was failing some sort of test. If this was a test, he hadn't studied for it and shouldn't be surprised he was failing. "You're the best, Z."

Zaina glance at the clock on the wall. "It's getting late, I should let you go."

"I hate to just leave. We should celebrate the success of your live stream idea. We could go get dessert?" Jasper offered.

Zaina yawned widely and covered her mouth. Jasper peered at her; he was almost certain she had just faked a yawn. Why would she do that?

"I'm going to have to take a rain check, Jasper. I've had a long day."

It was only nine p.m., but who was he to judge whether she was truly tired. "Do you need anything from me before I go?" he asked, still not wanting to leave her.

Zaina stretched her arms then rubbed her eyes. "No, I'm fine. I'll talk to you later." She walked over to a bookshelf next to her tea station and picked up a bag with a piece of paper stapled to it. She placed it on the counter. "Here is Jax's order."

Jasper put on his coat and zipped it. He pulled out his car keys and swung the key ring around his finger; he knew he was fidgeting to avoid feeling unbalanced, but he couldn't help himself. He swung the keys around and swallowed. "Have a good night, Z." He picked up the bag and left the store.

He drove home deflated and confused about how things had ended with Zaina. They'd had a great live, things were on track for his business, and she'd said her shop was going crazy with orders too, so what was the problem? Jasper didn't feel like making or getting anything for dinner, so he had a Greek yogurt with strawberries and sent a text to Jax to make sure closing went well at Hop's Heaven.

Later, he brushed his teeth, took a shower and put on lounge pants and a T-shirt. The evening with Zaina replayed in his head. Had he accidentally insulted her when he told her he'd give her a bonus when he had the investors he was seeking? Why had that made her mad? Or did it have to do with the cards? They seemed straightforward. Maybe he'd missed something. He rolled over and worked on turning off his brain so he could get some sleep.

Chapter Nineteen

♥

ZAINA

Zaina woke up annoyed. She knew she shouldn't have thought Jasper was interested in anything other than his future chain of breweries, but last night, he reminded her it was his number one concern. He'd listened to his tarot reading and all he'd thought was how the King of Pentacles meant riches. *Ugh. Men were the worst.* Why did she let herself think for one second Jasper had the potential to be any different?

Zaina looked in her fridge and saw she had a couple of eggs, a package of English muffins, and some deli ham. She decided to make a ham and egg sandwich but she wanted a cup of tea first. As her tea was steeping, her phone chimed. It was her mom calling. She was so glad she'd told her mom about her fake dating arrangement with Jasper after the Feel Good Friday show. Keeping stuff from her mom made her feel terrible. She unlocked her phone and answered it. "Hi, Mom! What's up?"

"Nothing much. How are you doing?"

"It's been super busy in the shop. I think I need to hire a part-timer to help."

"Wow, that's wonderful! I'm not surprised at all. You have such fun stuff in your shop."

"Thanks, Mom." Zaina took a sip of her tea. "Is something going on or did you just call to say hi?"

"Do I need an excuse to call my favorite daughter?"

"No, of course not, but you tend to have a reason when you call."

Zaina's mom, Amy, chuckled. "You got me. I called to talk to you about something. It's kind of funny, really."

Zaina pulled out her iron skillet, added a pat of butter, and turned on the heat. "I'm listening."

"You know how Mark doesn't really use social media?"

"Mm-hmm," Zaina said as she cracked an egg in her pan.

"He has accounts. He just doesn't really use them very much. I was on the iPad at home, and I watched the video you made with Jasper on your date."

"You did? This feels kind of awkward now."

"You should feel awkward. That video is loaded with sexual tension. You two are practically eye fu—"

"Mom!"

"I'm just telling it like it is."

Zaina pulled out a spatula and carefully flipped her egg. She wanted her egg to be a little runny when she put it on the English muffin. "You were watching the video. What does that have to do with Mark?"

"I commented on your video, and I didn't realize the iPad was logged into Mark's account."

"That doesn't sound like a big deal, unless Mark didn't like that?"

"I'm sure he won't care. I don't think people even realize it's his account. He hasn't posted in ages. It looks like a fake account. I haven't mentioned it to him yet because I just figured out what happened this morning."

Zaina separated the English muffin and put it in her toaster. As it toasted, she turned off the egg and put a couple of slices on Deli Ham on top of it. She took out a plate and added a handful of blackberries to it. "How did you figure it out?"

"I was putting some books on hold via the library website, and I got a notification that I had a direct message from Jasper Kane!"

Zaina's English muffins popped up. Distracted, she pulled them out with her fingers, burning them and dropped the English muffins on her countertop. "Ouch, ouch" she said.

"Honey, are you okay?" her mom immediately asked.

"I'm fine. I burned my fingers getting the English muffin out of the toaster."

"Did you try blowing on them?"

"Doing that right now, Mom."

Zaina blew on her hand as her mom read her the message Jasper had sent.

"Sounds like Jasper would really like to meet Mark," Amy said.

Zaina put the English muffin on her plate and then used a spatula to take the egg and ham stack and place it on the bottom half of the muffin. Her mouth watered as she put the top on her sandwich and took a bite. "One sec," she mumbled as she chewed her food. She swallowed and spoke to her mom.

"I'm sure he would love that. I think all he cares about is having his brewery become a chain," Zaina said dryly.

"Zaina, that is not all he cares about! I could tell when I met him at the live remote that he cares about you, and it's even more clear when you two post your videos."

"Mom, that's acting. It's all part of our deal."

"Zaina, I hear what you are saying, but that's not what my eyes are seeing. I can feel it in my gut. He likes you."

Zaina took another bite of her food. She needed time to think. "Mom, I would be thrilled to find out that Jasper was more interested in me than just as a business partner. I'd want to date him if I could know he would put me, us, above his desire for business success. That's just not him. Jasper was raised in a family that only cares about having more money than everyone else around them. He's been working for years to get his family's approval and if he can get investors to help back his franchise plan, he'll have the success and the approval he's so desperate for."

"Zaina, in the last seven years with Mark, I've learned there can be a balance between a successful spouse's work life and having a family."

"I don't think it's the same, Mom. Mark was already the CEO of ADM Investments when you met him, and he didn't have an overbearing family growing up."

"I know it's not the same. What I'm trying to say is maybe it doesn't have to be massive business success or you."

Zaina took her half-eaten sandwich and used it to sop up the runny egg on her plate before it got to her blackberries. She took time to mull over what her mom was saying and her need to know whether Jasper was a Kane through and through or if maybe he would choose a full life over a life of work. "Mom, I think I know what to do, but I'm going to need your help."

"How can I help, honey?"

"Can you show Mark the message from Jasper and ask him to set up a meeting?"

"Are you sure that's what you want to do?"

"Yes. Please ask Mark if he will set up a meeting with Jasper."

"I'm sure he'll be happy to meet Jasper. Mark has been interested in the craft beer industry. He loves trying different local beers, and he mentioned something about what a fast-growing industry it is, and that man loves to be invested in businesses on the cusp of something big. I know Jasper will really appreciate you helping him to get this meeting. I know I didn't mention Mark to him when I met him. Did you tell him Mark is your stepdad?"

"Nope. And I'm not going to."

"Wait, you're asking for this meeting, but you aren't going to tell Jasper who Mark is to you?"

"No. Don't you see? This way, I can see how important I am to him."

"Zaina, hon, I don't follow."

"If he meets with Mark and things go well and he goes forward with his expansion dreams, then I know what matters most to him and it wouldn't be me."

"Zaina, are you sure you want to do this? It seems like you are trying to trick Jasper. There isn't anything wrong with being a successful businessperson."

"I know that, Mom, but think of this. I need someone who will put our family first. I will not tie myself to someone who is going to always be gone working. I want a husband and a father for my children, who will be home nights and weekends. Otherwise, I don't need to bother with having a husband. I can have a child on my own. Like you did."

"Zaina, you know that was a very different time back then. I was 16, my parents were very strict and—please don't take this the wrong way—I didn't have access to an abortion, or to be more correct, I thought I didn't have any access."

"Mom, I don't take it the wrong way. I understand, especially having lived through my teen years, I have so much respect for you. I don't know how you did it and I don't think that I could have and I'm so glad you were there to take me to get birth control back then."

"Thank you, honey, I'm glad you understand. I don't get why you want to test Jasper and I don't like this, but I'll talk to Mark today about setting up a meeting with him."

"Mom, if this is a total disaster, you can tell me I told you so."

"Let the record reflect. I get an 'I told you so' when this plan of yours backfires."

"Love you, Mom!"

"I love you, Zaina. Bye."

Chapter Twenty

♥

JASPER

On a typical day, Jasper's mind was occupied with beer: what the status was of the current beers on tap, what was brewing and what he could do to grow his Hop's Heaven business. Lately, things had not been typical and more of his mind was occupied with the beautiful and vexing Zaina. He'd tossed and turned most of the night, trying to figure out what he needed to do to fix things so they could go back to sexy flirting and genuine conversations.

Over the years, he'd had his share of women and then some, but this was the first time he felt like he was out of his depth. Usually, he knew exactly what to say and do to please a woman. After yesterday, it was very clear that he did not know how to please Zaina. Well, when it came to sex, he'd learned she shivered when he kissed that freckle next to her belly button. That he knew. It was her mind he didn't get. She wanted something from him. What was it? Did he even have it to give to her? His shoulders slumped, and he leaned back in his office chair. He needed to get back to what he was good at, which was beer, and stop obsessing over Zaina.

Jasper turned on his work computer and waited for it to load. Maybe today he'd make progress on potential investor meetings. One nice thing about having done the live last night was he didn't have to spend a sizeable chunk of today rewatching videos of Zaina's beautiful brown eyes looking at him like she cared about him. Jasper pulled up his email and started responding to a few work messages that had come in. Since they'd been doing their viral fake dating, he'd gotten a few requests from restaurants to see if he distributed his beer.

Once he was done, he checked the Hop's Heaven Instagram account. It had over a thousand notifications and that caused him to almost overlook a new message. He clicked opened the Meta Business Suite and went to his inbox. There, amid hundreds of spam messages, was a reply from Mark Anderson. He rubbed his eyes. Jasper couldn't believe what he was seeing.

Dear Jasper:

I'd be interested in hearing more about your franchise business plan. Please contact my executive assistant at 773-555-1212 so we can schedule a meeting.

Regards,

Mark Anderson

ADM Investments

Jasper jumped out of his seat! He could not believe Mark Anderson wanted to meet with him. The CEO of the largest venture capital firm in Illinois was interested in his business plan! He had a lump in his throat. He'd been working for a decade toward this day.

First things first, he opened the calendar app on his phone. Oh, who was he kidding? He'd take a meeting with ADM Investments any day of the week, any time of the day. Nothing else could change his life like this meeting could. He unlocked his phone and as he dialed the number, he had a panicked thought. What if this was all part of a scam? What if he thought he was calling Mark's executive assistant, and it was really some hacker?

He reread the message. Almost anything could be spam, but usually those messages had spelling, grammar, or context errors. He was not crazy to think this was real, and why wouldn't it be? Jasper's business was solid and could be a smart investment, that's what all his years of work had built. Buoyed by his thoughts, he unlocked his phone and dialed the executive assistant's phone number.

The phone rang twice.

"ADM Investments, Mark Anderson's office," a pleasant older woman's voice answered.

"Hi, my name is Jasper Kane. I received a message from Mr. Anderson. He asked me to call you and set up a meeting."

"Thanks for contacting us so quickly. Mr. Anderson would like to meet you and tour your brewery. He's going out of town on Thursday. Would you be available on Tuesday or Wednesday?"

Jasper's heart was racing. "Either day is good for me."

"Alright, let me just double check here. Does Wednesday at two p.m. work for you?"

"Perfect."

"Excellent. Then expect Mr. Anderson at two p.m. and if you don't have any conflicts, I'll schedule this meeting to end at four."

"That sounds great. There will be plenty of time for questions and for me to give Mr. Anderson a tour of Hop's Heaven."

"Is this the best number for you, Mr. Kane?"

"Yes, this is my cell phone."

"I'll pass on your number and Mr. Anderson will see you this Wednesday. If something comes up and you need to reschedule, please contact me right away."

"Thank you very much. Please thank Mr. Anderson for this opportunity."

"I will. Have a good day."

"Thanks, you too!"

Jasper clicked to end the call, and then he let out a whoop of joy. The day after tomorrow, Mark Anderson would be here! Jasper grinned from ear to ear. His fake dating plan had actually worked! When he'd come up with this harebrained scheme, even he hadn't believed it would lead to an investor, let alone one of the biggest venture capital firms in the country and certainly the biggest headquartered in Chicago. He was so excited; he wanted to tell everyone, including his mother. This meeting was an accomplishment that she would understand and approve of.

He probably should wait until after the meeting to say anything to his mother, but he couldn't help himself. He unlocked his phone and clicked on his mom's contact info. *Wait a second, what the heck am I doing?* He smashed the end call button and threw down his phone. She was the last person he should share this good news with. He'd been working so hard all his adult life to become his own person and not live by his parent's values and here he was running to call his mom because he was on the cusp of a life-changing business deal. It was as if he'd forgotten all the times she'd belittled his brewery. Major bullet dodged, Jasper scrolled up to Sean's number and hit the call button.

"Hey, pal. What's up?" Sean answered.

"Hi Sean, are you still planning on coming up here for our Monday lunch?"

"You know it. I've been working on mini-Italian beef sandwiches for the Superbowl buffet. You want to try a few varieties today?"

"Sean, have I ever said no to trying anything you cook?"

"Now that you mention it, no, you have not."

"Great, I'll see you soon, buddy." Jasper ended the call. He looked at his phone. Should he call Zaina? Yesterday she would have been the first person he told, but after last night, he wasn't sure where he stood with her. Then again, this would not have happened without her part in the viral marketing campaign.

He sent her a text.

> JASPER: Hey Z, I hope you are having a good day.

He rolled his eyes and deleted his partial text.

> JASPER: Z,

He paused, unsure of what to say. Once again, Zaina had him so wound up, he didn't know which way was up. Jasper's chest tightened, and he clenched his jaw. He didn't like the uncertainty of not knowing where he stood with Zaina. At least in the past, he'd known he was at the top of her shit list. Now he thought he was back on it, but this time, he truly did not know why.

He still wanted to tell her the good news, so he pushed aside his uncertainty and wrote a new text.

> JASPER: Zaina, our fake dating has been a amazing success! The biggest venture capital company in our area reached out to me and I have a meeting scheduled for Wednesday with the CEO. I could not have done this without you!

He reread his text, and he still felt good about it, so he hit send. He'd been revising and polishing his plan for three years now. Jasper got up to go work in the brewhouse. As he went about his work, he looked at each inch of his establishment through the eyes of a potential investor. Every speck of dust and smudge on steel needed to be cleaned up before Mark arrived. The next forty-eight hours were going to be rough, but he'd go without sleep and pay overtime for staff to make sure that he put his best foot forward for this meeting. Soon he got lost in his cleaning.

"Hey Jasper," Jax said.

Jasper jumped and turned around.

"Hi, Jax. Sorry, you startled me."

"Sean is in the taproom; I figured I come get you."

"He's here already?

Jax checked their digital watch. "It's almost two p.m., Jasp."

"Holy smokes, it was only eleven five minutes ago."

Jax shook their head, and their braid swished from side to side. "Sean's food smells amazing. You better hurry before me and Kathy eat everything Sean brought for us."

"I'm going to go to wash up and then I'll be right over, so save some food for me."

Jasper went and washed his hands and then walked over to where Sean was sitting at the bar and clasped his best friend on the shoulder. "Sean, my man, thanks for saving us from starvation!"

"It's my pleasure. I hope you're hungry!"

"I've been working my ass off all morning in the brewhouse. I've got news buddy, monumental news!"

Sean uncovered the containers of Italian beef, peppers, provolone cheese, and fresh baked rolls. He handed Jasper and Jax a plate, then he looked over his shoulder at Kathy, who had her gray hair up in a messy bun complete with a pencil to keep it in place. She was furiously typing on her laptop. "Hey Kathy, you want some beef?"

Kathy didn't even pause in her typing as she replied, "I'd love some Sean!"

Sean turned back to Jasper, who was already chowing down on his first sandwich. "I'm going to bring her a plate, then you can tell me all about your news."

Jasper nodded and continued eating. "What do you think, Jax?"

"I think this is the best Italian beef I've ever had in my life." Jax said as they chomped.

"I think you're right, Jax. What beer would you pair with this?"

Jax rubbed their tattooed left arm sleeve in thought. "Jasper, I've gotta say, I think everything except the dark chocolate stout works with this meal."

"I think that's exactly right. Hey, can you pour me a five-ounce Lupercalia Lager?"

"Sure thing, boss." Jax poured the beer and handed it to Jasper.

Sean sat down next to Jasper. "What do y'all think?"

"Jax says it's the best Italian beef they've ever had."

"And you?"

"Sean, the seasoning blend is perfect, the broth has a little brine, and I can taste rosemary, thyme and oregano. The roll is so soft and fluffy, the whole sandwich is practically melting in my mouth." Jasper finished his review by leaning over and kissing his best friend's cheek. "That's a chef's kiss for you!"

Sean knocked his shoulder into his friend. "Now tell me about your big news."

"I have a meeting with a potential investor on Wednesday."

"That's fantastic buddy! I know you'll knock it out of the park. You've put in all the work and you've got your ducks in a row. I've known since the first time I met you; you were destined for big things. One day, just a few years from now, Nicole and I will be on a vacation out in Arizona or maybe Oklahoma and we will stop in the local Hop's Heaven for some tasty beer!"

Jasper smiled widely. "I'm loving this scenario. I'm picturing a minivan, and a cute little dog, maybe a Corgi or a Yorkshire Terrier? Sean and Nicole traveling Route 66 going to all sorts of diners along the way."

Sean laughed, "That sounds like a fantastic plan. I'll tell Nicole we need to look at minivans. Maybe we could even get a paper map to hang on the wall and plan our trip."

"Be like Zaina and I and go viral. People love travel content."

"Now we're talking! We can make content, talk about food and Jesse's Pub and write off the entire trip."

Jasper tapped his temple. "That's me, always thinking about the angles."

"Speaking of you and Zaina, how's everything going? Nicole made me watch that live and once again, you two look very cozy. And that tarot card reading. Sounds like you have a decision to make."

"I didn't know you were into that woo-woo stuff, Sean."

"Well, I wouldn't say into it, but I guess I take Zaina's readings to heart."

"Huh, well I don't. Then again, she showed that king of pentacles card, and now I have a meeting with a potential investor. Maybe there is something to it?"

"Or maybe it means you need to decide if what's going on between you and Zaina is for show or if you two are really into each other?"

Jasper rubbed his chest; he felt a slight twinge there. Was his heart trying to tell him to listen to Sean? "I don't think Zaina is interested in me. She's good at acting."

"Dude, I don't think anyone is that good at acting."

"You really think so?" Jasper hated to get his hopes up, especially with Zaina.

"Mark my words, Zaina is into you, just as much as you are into her." Sean said.

"Now that's really hard for me to believe," Jasper sighed. "Sean, let's go back to talking about my big meeting on Wednesday. My fake dating life is bumming me out."

"Sure thing, Jasp."

Jasper appreciated Sean sticking around and letting him walk through his plan for the meeting, from giving his two cents on the font of his business plan PowerPoint to role playing being Mark for a tour of the brewery.

Chapter Twenty-One

♥

ZAINA

Zaina was in her shop ordering shipping supplies for the second time in a few weeks, which was an outstanding problem to have. She'd put up a help wanted sign in the window, but so far, no one was biting. She should probably take the time to post online in the Marley Creek Community group. There must be someone who was looking for a part-time job. In the meantime, she also needed to find the time to make more oils to sell in the shop and on Etsy. Not only were the sex and success oils flying off the shelves, but she'd also been getting so many requests for hex breaking soap. She wasn't sure what was out there in the world, but people were feeling cursed.

Zaina's stomach rumbled, and then her phone rang. She looked at the display; it was her stepdad, Mark. She unlocked her phone and answered.

"Hi, Mark!"

"Hey Zaina, I've got a meeting with Jasper Kane today in Marley Creek, so I was thinking I'd swing by after. Maybe we can get some pizza?"

"Any excuse for Best Pizza Near Me right?"

"I've been trying to do the low carb thing and I'm due for a cheat meal, and Best Pizza Near Me is the best pizza around, bar none." Mark confided.

"I better go see if I have pickles on hand."

"This is why you are my favorite stepdaughter."

"I'm the only one! You and my mom with your jokes. You two really are made for each other." She laughed.

"Do you want me to bring any beer from Hop's Heaven?"

"Totally your call."

"Okay, then if I see something that sounds good with pizza, I'll get some to go."

"That sounds great. I'll see you later, Mark."

"Bye, Z."

Zaina clicked off her phone and took a deep breath. The meeting was definitely happening. Her heart sank; she'd really hoped that Jasper would have chosen her over his business, but he was a Kane, and Kane's were all about how much money they could accumulate. It was nice while it lasted. They'd had their fun and at least now she knew where he stood.

He was only interested in her as a means to an end. Jasper had made that clear when they started this fake relationship. Things had just gotten murky along the way, and she'd let herself believe they could have something real. When they were together, he made her feel, and she knew this sounded so trite, but he made her feel special. Like he believed in her. She'd thought he looked at her differently, but maybe she had misunderstood him and misread the situation.

She told herself she wished him well today, but if he offered her a bonus again, she would not take it. The thought of him landing a deal and then writing her a big check made her stomach churn. It didn't even make sense. The whole point of this thing was to get enough money to pay for the cost of going through artificial insemination and all that could entail. The thought of him giving her more than they'd agreed upon made her want to puke. It was nonsensical, but that was how she felt. As far as she was concerned, he could live his dream and have as many Hop's Heavens across America as there were McDonalds.

Now that it was clear where Jasper's heart lay, it was time for her to move on and refocus on her dream. She didn't need him. What she needed to do was remember why she'd agreed to this in the first place and stop having fantasies about an actual relationship with Jasper. She played with her earring and tried to refocus on her work. As she was printing out labels for today's batch of shipments, the store bell chimed, and a woman walked in.

She was a few inches taller than Zaina, which wasn't saying much since Zaina was just a little over five feet tall. She had red hair that Zaina could tell in an instant was all natural. Her pale face was covered with freckles, and she had on glasses that had fallen down her nose. She pushed them up on her face and approached Zaina at the counter.

"Um, hi. I was wondering if you are still hiring?"

Zaina nodded her head. "Yes, would you like an application?"

"That would be great."

Zaina pulled out a clipboard and a pen with a flower top. She took one application she'd printed off earlier in the week and put it on the clipboard and handed it to the woman.

"You can have a seat over there in the reading nook and fill out the application and bring it back up to me. Do you have time for an interview today?"

The woman's eyes widened. "Oh, wow, that would be great, actually."

Zaina held out her hand. "I'm Zaina Evans. This is my store."

The woman's ears reddened. "I follow you on social media, so I feel like I know you already."

Zaina smiled, "Wow, this is a first. I don't know how I feel about this?"

"M-my name is Hannah Taylor."

"Great to meet you, Hannah. Take your time filling out the application, and if you have questions, just let me know."

Zaina went back to organizing today's shipments. Fed Ex would be at her store shortly. She wondered how things were going over at Hop's Heaven. She didn't spend enough time with Mark to know if he would wind up investing in Jasper's business, but she appreciated that he'd set up the meeting. It stung, but she had wanted to know where Jasper's loyalties lay. Distracted, she sighed loudly, and Hannah's head jerked up. Zaina mouthed sorry and felt a flush of embarrassment. She didn't want to scare off the only person who seemed to be interested in the job.

Hannah walked back over to the counter and handed Zaina her completed application. Zaina reviewed it and tried to remember where she'd put the list of interview questions she'd typed up. She opened her file drawer and flipped through, looking for the one that said *Interviews*. She didn't find it. Not wanting to waste Hannah's time, she figured she'd wing it. She picked up her favorite pen and the clipboard with the application and said to Hannah, "Let's go sit and have a chat."

They sat in the reading nook, and Zaina looked down at the application. Hannah perched on the edge of the chair, her legs together, and turned to the side. She sat very straight and had her hands folded in her lap.

"It looks like you're new to Marley Creek?" Zaina asked.

"Yes, I moved here six months ago," Hannah replied.

"Are you looking for specific hours?"

"I'm open."

"Right now, I need someone who can work about twenty hours a week and who will be available at least one weekend day."

Hannah nodded. "That's no problem."

"Tell me about your retail experience," Zaina said.

"I've worked in a clothing store, a bakery and a bookstore. I currently work at a grocery store."

"When you worked in the bookstore, did you ship orders?"

"Yes, all the time. I've worked with a few types of point of sales. When I worked in the bakery, we served a variety of teas and coffees, so I have experience in that as well," Hannah explained.

With each answer Hannah gave, Zaina was more excited about Hannah working for her. "Hannah, everything looks good, and I could really use the help as soon as possible. Assuming your references check out, how soon could you start?"

"Honestly, I could start this afternoon." Hannah said. Zaina noticed she was clenching her hands together tightly.

"Then I better check these references," Zaina tapped the clipboard. She stood up. "I'll call you by Friday to let you know either way."

Hannah stood up. She smoothed her pants and licked her dry lips.

Zaina started walking to the door, and Hannah followed her. At the door, Zaina turned and put out her hand. "It was a pleasure to meet you. I'll be in touch."

Hannah gave Zaina a firm handshake and left.

Zaina pulled out her cell phone and began checking Hannah's references. She wanted to get this taken care of as soon as possible, especially since she didn't know how soon Mark would be here and because she had the feeling Hannah needed her more than she needed Hannah.

Just after four p.m. Mark walked into New Age Stones and Witch Crafts. He was wearing a tailored suit, his tie loosened, and carrying a box of Best Pizza Near Me.

He smiled his dazzling smile, the one that made everyone say he looked like an actor. When she was pressed, Zaina would admit it was still wild to her that her mom, Amy Evans, a registered nurse, who had dated no one while Zaina was growing up, had wound up married to a mega rich guy with movie star looks that was twelve years younger than her. Even parents can surprise you.

"You've got pickles, right?"

Zaina crossed her arms. "Do I have pickles? Of course I do. What's a pizza without pickles?"

"Not as good as it could be, that's for sure." Mark said. He looked around the store, "How's things? Any landlord stuff I need to know about?"

"No, everything is wonderful. Heat works, no plumbing problems."

"Did you want to eat down here so you can stay open?"

"I can close early. I don't have any clients coming to pick up anything and I rarely have foot traffic on Wednesday evenings in February. Actually, I have little foot traffic outside special events in February."

"I'm sure things will perk up." Mark said.

Zaina turned the open sign to closed and locked the front door. "Online, things have been going gangbusters. I've had more orders over the last few weeks than I had during the entire holiday season, and I had a good holiday season!"

"And all that is because of the videos you and Jasper have been making, huh?"

Zaina nodded, and her stomach roiled. She wanted and didn't want to know how the meeting went. "Ready to head upstairs?" She asked.

"I'm starving; let's go."

They walked upstairs to Zaina's apartment. Mark set down the pizza and pulled two cans of beer out of his suit jacket. "I wasn't sure what beer you preferred. Take either. I'm going to wash my hands."

Zaina washed her hands at the kitchen sink and then set the table with a couple of plates, napkins, and two mason jars of water. Last, she pulled out a jar of pickles and set it on the table. Sweat beaded on her back. She was getting more and more eager to find out how the meeting went and if Mark was going to be investing in Hop's Heaven.

Mark came back from the bathroom. He took off his suit jacket and folded it over, placing it on Zaina's recliner.

He popped the top on his beer and took a long drink. Zaina opened the pizza box, and they both put pizza on their plates. Once Mark had added pickles on top of his pizza, he took a bite and moaned. "The best pizza anywhere. Sometimes I think we should sell the condo downtown and move here just so we can have Best Pizza Near Me delivered. Then, of course, your mom reminds me she loves the city."

"I bet if you offer to tip enough, They will deliver to you."

"True, they probably would, but it still feels wrong."

Zaina took a big gulp of her Lupercalia Lager and steeled herself to ask Mark about the meeting. "How did the meeting go? Are you going to invest in Jasper's business?"

Mark set down his pizza. "Zaina, why didn't you tell Jasper you asked me to set up the meeting?"

The pizza and beer began turning in her stomach. "I, uh," she looked at the floor. "I thought it would be better if he didn't know we were related."

Mark shook his head, "I have to say, that was not very nice. I didn't know that he didn't know you were my stepdaughter, and that you asked to set up the meeting. When we met and I told him how instrumental you were in getting him and I connected, he was stunned, and I felt like an ass. I love you, Zaina, but never make me look like a jerk again." His eyes bored into hers, and she noticed his jaw was clenched.

Zaina could barely get a breath in, sweat sprouted under her arms, and she could feel heat rising up her neck.

"I'm sorry, Mark. I didn't think about how it would make you look."

Mark nodded, "Thank you, but I'm surprised you didn't think about how Jasper might feel. You're usually someone who considers other people's feelings."

Zaina felt a twinge in her chest. She wasn't used to anyone calling her out on her behavior. Usually, there was no need. She hung her head. She really wanted this conversation to be over, but part of her had to know what happened with the deal. She plowed ahead.

"How did the meeting go?"

"Once he knew that you and I were related, by marriage, but still related, he said he didn't know if it would be right for him to try and convince me to invest in his business."

Zaina scrunched up her face. "He did?"

Mark took a big bite of pizza and chewed. When he was done, he responded. "Yes, said it seemed like a conflict of interest for him."

Zaina sat slack-jawed. "Huh."

"Exactly. Care to share why he might feel like that?"

Zaina raised her shoulder and took a drink of her beer.

"You know I could keep harping on you right now, but I will not do that. You know why?"

Zaina shook her head.

"Because I remember the foolishness Amy and I got up to when we weren't ready to admit we were crazy about each other."

"W-what? T-that's just…"

Mark leaned back in his chair. "Please go on, tell me how none of this has to do with you two having big feelings for each other, or we can let it lie and enjoy the rest of our pizza and talk about Julian for a while."

Zaina ate some of her pizza and tried to gather her thoughts and emotions. Was Jasper into her? Had she made a huge mistake? Then she spoke, "So is Julian going to play T-ball this spring?"

"This will be the first year he's old enough to play regular baseball," Mark replied.

Chapter
Twenty-Two

♥

JASPER

Jasper was so mad; he didn't trust himself to be around people. "Jax, I'm taking the rest of the night off."

Jax nodded and poured a beer for a plumber sitting at the end of the bar.

Jasper walked out to his car, got in and let loose a primal scream. He hit the steering wheel with his fist over and over What was Zania up to? Why would she set him up like that? Was this some sort of long revenge scheme she'd been working on or weeks to get him back for being an asshole to her in school? He'd thought she liked him! At the very least, he thought they had had an honest relationship. Turns out he was very wrong. She'd set him up good. He'd been so excited for this meeting with Mark, a meeting that he'd thought he'd made happen because of the work he'd been putting in over the years and their viral campaign.

Mark had only met with him because Zaina had asked him to. Good lord, he'd had a pity meeting. What a joke he was. Thank God he hadn't told his mother. At least now he knew where he stood with Zaina. She must truly hate him; that was the only explanation he could come up with. He felt like such an idiot for telling her how excited he was about the meeting with Mark and how he'd give her a bonus for all her help when he landed an investor. He'd gone on about Mark and ADM investments—he'd mansplained her stepfather's business and she'd said nothing.

His face burned with embarrassment, and he clenched his jaw so tight, he was afraid he was going to crack a molar. He needed to burn off some of this anger and soon. He got out of his car and checked his trunk. Thank God his workout clothes were in there. He got back in his car and drove over to the gym. He needed to hit something until his brain turned off.

Two hours later, Jasper opened his front door and slowly made his way up to his bedroom. If all went as planned, he'd be so sore from hitting the bag at the gym and running six miles on the treadmill that Zaina's face wouldn't be able to creep into his mind. He checked his phone to see if Zaina had called or texted him with an explanation for her behavior. A small part of him hoped this was all some sort of silly mix-up and Zaina hadn't acted maliciously. He had racked his brain trying to come up with an innocent excuse for Zaina not telling him.

Jasper recalled Sean telling him that when he'd first dated Nicole, he'd accidentally forgot to hit the send button on an important text and that had almost ended their relationship before it had really begun. Maybe Zaina had thought she'd mentioned Mark was her stepfather. His heart sank. Who was he kidding? They had talked about Mark and ADM Investments, and Zaina said nothing. Why had she set up the meeting and not told him? His head was pounding from the way he'd had his jaw clenched for hours now. He would be lucky if he didn't grind his teeth into dust tonight. Of course, even with the long workout, he had his doubts that he'd be able to sleep well tonight. One thing he knew was it was time to rethink their fake relationship. He was done.

The next day, Jasper committed to focusing on his business. As the day went on, his muscles began to ache in a delayed reaction to his intense workout the night before. He refused to take acetaminophen, wanting the soreness to distract him from the pain that Zaina had caused him. Once the taproom was closed he should have just gone home, but he didn't feel like driving home to his big empty home.

Zaina had changed something in him, and he'd thought they'd begun building a relationship. He'd enjoyed having a partner, even if it had begun as a viral marketing stunt. He scrolled through his email. If another potential investor contacted him today, he wasn't even sure he would bother to respond. What was the point of anything when you couldn't trust people? He looked over at the futon and memories of being iced-in with Zaina and the time they'd shared flooded him. He needed to get rid of the brewery or the futon. The ache in his heart continued to grow, dragging him under.

He remembered how Zaina had looked at him that night, like she finally forgave him for treating her like crap in high school. The way she'd been so bold. Every time he looked at the futon, he could taste her on his tongue and heard her screaming his name as she came. The futon needed to go, now. Jasper tossed the throw pillows off it, then pulled the mattress off the wooden frame and dragged it through the brewhouse and out to his dumpster.

Jasper threw open the top of the dumpster, which had just been emptied earlier. He folded the mattress in half and picked it up. Grunting, he lifted it up high enough to rest it on the metal rim. He took a breath and then, with a yell, he pushed it in, then he stalked back inside the brewhouse. He walked to the corner of the warehouse, where he'd installed a fire ax alongside an industrial fire extinguisher. He pulled the ax off the wall and walked back to his office.

His shoulders and arms were no longer aching from yesterday's workout. Right now, his body was filled with anger. He paused for a moment, gripping the ax with both hands. When Mark had said Zaina had set up the meeting, his eyes had stung. He'd almost cried in front of fucking Mark Anderson. His face burned with embarrassment. He swung the ax, irrevocably damaging the frame. Over and over, he swung the ax, reducing the futon frame to a pile of kindling. Sweat poured down his face, and he pulled up his T-shirt and wiped it off.

He put the ax back where it belonged and picked up a pair of gloves from the brewhouse. He pulled a plastic garbage can out of the taproom and filled it with wood. By the time he'd finished the last trash can load of wood, his adrenaline and his anger had waned. His muscles ached from swinging the ax, but he felt better than he had since the completed debacle of a meeting. Jasper got the broom and dustpan and finished cleaning his now spacious office. He yawned, grateful that his meltdown had resulted in finally getting his mind to shut up about Zaina. He could go home, show and fall into bed. Tomorrow, he'd send her a text message and end their arrangement. *It's better this happened now, before I really fell in love with her.*

Chapter Twenty-Three

♥

ZAINA

Zaina hated going to the grocery store, and she tried to put it off as long as she could. Her emergency roll of toilet paper was almost gone, so she was going to have to go to the store after she closed New Aged Stones and Witch Crafts for the day. It was below freezing, but at least the days were getting longer. This time next month, the sun would still be up when she finished her workday.

She probably should have made a grocery list, but she'd been too distracted by her disappointment in Jasper. Plus, he'd had the nerve to not contact her at all since he'd met with Mark. She didn't even know if they were still fake dating, and frankly, she didn't care if they were. She didn't need the dating; he'd already agreed to pay for her medical bills and she knew even if they didn't finish the whole contract that he'd keep up his end of the bargain. Zaina parked her car and got a shopping cart out of the cart corral. At least it was a Saturday night, not a Saturday morning.

The parking lot was nearly empty. Anyone who had a life would not be at the grocery store tonight. She wandered up and down the aisles picking foods that appealed to her at the moment. *I really should have eaten before coming here.* She looked down at her cart. What else did she need? She had cereal, a blue box of mac and cheese, and a couple of bags of salad. Oh yes, she needed toilet paper. It would be a serious problem if she left this store without getting that. She could always order out for food. She turned away from the front of the store and headed back toward the soap and sundries area.

On her way, she passed the beer aisle. Porters, stouts, lagers, IPAs, non-alcoholic beers, there were so many brands. As she continued on, she saw a cooler in front of her with a hand lettered sign: Try a local beer! Zaina looked at the beers in the cooler. She hadn't realized there were so many breweries in her area. She opened the cooler door and looked inside. If they carried Jasper's beer, she might get some to keep in her fridge. The man made some tasty brews. She checked and double checked, but she didn't see any. Out of the corner of her eye, she saw someone approaching her. She turned her head towards the person when she heard the unmistakable voice of Jasper on his cell phone. "Sean, what did you say was the best cut to grill, chuck roast?" Zaina kept her head down and carefully maneuvered her cart forward so that she could escape down the next aisle before Jasper could see her. What were the odds he'd be shopping on a Saturday night? Shouldn't he be in Hop's Heaven? Since when did he have a Saturday night off?

Zaina knew her anger was irrational, and it was because of her feeling uncomfortable about running into Jasper. If this had happened a week ago, she'd be trying to help him with his shopping, even though she hated the grocery store and didn't cook. Fortunately, she was now in the toilet paper aisle and she couldn't hear Jasper talking anymore. She tossed the first pack of toilet paper into her cart and made a beeline for fifteen items or fewer check out. She tossed her groceries onto the belt and took out her debit card. If she wasn't in desperate need of groceries, she would have abandoned her shopping cart and left the store as soon as she realized Jasper was here.

"Do you have a preferred card?" a familiar voice said. Zaina looked up and saw the red hair of Hannah.

"Hi Zaina, do you have a preferred card?"

Zaina pulled out her keychain. "That's right, you had Diamond's listed as your current job."

Hannah scanned Zaina's keycard and handed her keys back to her.

"And here I am," she said and started scanning Zaina's items.

Zaina leaned in toward Hannah conspiratorially. "It's kind of a long story, but I'm in a hurry. Can you scan faster?"

Hannah frowned. "Sure, but is this because I didn't get the job? You can just tell me that. It won't be the first time I've heard I didn't get the job."

Zaina waved her hands, "It's not that at all! I've been waiting for a call back from here to verify your employment, but since I'm here and I can see you are working with my own eyes, I'd say that box is checked."

Hannah bit her lip, but she couldn't stop her smile. "Your total is thirty-six dollars and fifty-four cents."

Zaina swiped her card while Hannah bagged her groceries. "Can you start on Monday?"

Hannah smiled widely and her eyes lit up. "What time?"

"How's nine o'clock? That will give us an hour to take care of the new employee paperwork before the store opens at ten a.m."

"Yes, of course, thank you so much Ms. Evans. I promise I'm a quick learner."

"Call me Zaina. No need for formality."

"Thank you, Zaina. I'll see you on Monday." Hanna put Zaina's bags into her shopping cart.

Zaina gripped the handle and began rushing out of the checkout. "I'm looking forward to us working together! Bye Hannah!"

Zaina's heart was beating out of her chest. She had to get the stuff in her car before Jasper left the store; she was parked too close to the only exit. She popped her trunk as she sped toward her car and then threw the groceries inside. She should have gotten a bottle of wine; too late now. There was no way she was going back inside Diamond's. She was breathing hard when she got in the driver's seat. She put on her seatbelt, started the car, and peeled out of the parking lot. In her rear-view mirror, she saw the store door *woosh* open and Jasper strode out carrying a reusable shopping bag in each hand. She felt a pang in her heart. She slowed down to a reasonable speed and drove home in silence.

Once she was home, she put away her groceries and started making the boxed macaroni and cheese. She avoided Jasper for the day, but she needed to be realistic. Marley Creek wasn't a place where it was easy to avoid someone completely. And it was even less so when you had friends in common. To keep ducking Jasper was untenable. She needed to suck it up and just text him because this was getting silly. Her water was boiling so she turned her attention to making her dinner and told herself she would contact Jasper tomorrow; no sense in doing it now. He probably had plans with his bags of food. Maybe he'd already replaced her.

She ripped open the box and macaroni flew all over her kitchen. She was fine. Everything was just fine. Zaina turned off the pot of water and got out her broom to sweep up her dinner. Good thing she'd bought some cereal and milk. Zaina didn't understand why Jasper was vexing her. She was more upset over him being the way he always was and focusing on money than she had been about Mike's cheating. She poured cereal into her bowl and then added milk. She took a bite and wished she'd gotten a banana to slice into it. Zaina also wished she was having whatever Jasper might make for dinner. If he had Sean coaching him, it was bound to be delicious and certainly not cold cereal for dinner. The cereal now tasted like cardboard in her mouth.

She wasn't entirely sure if she'd done the right thing by Jasper. Maybe she should have told him she knew Mark. But if she had done that, she'd be wondering if his interest in her was because of her connection to Mark. At least now she knew whatever he'd felt hadn't been clouded by what he could get out of her. She sighed. Why couldn't she meet a nice guy who wanted to settle down and have a family here in Marley Creek? Why did she keep dating the wrong guys? Even her fake dating had been a disaster. That was it. This time, she was going to stick to her plan and not date anyone. Being a single mom would be enough for her. She'd tried, but she could not put her trust in Jasper. Zaina decided to distract herself by watching a political thriller. She would wait until tomorrow to text Jasper.

Chapter
Twenty-Four

❤

JASPER

Jasper rolled over and looked at his phone. It was three a.m. He'd been tossing and turning since midnight. Against his better judgement, he picked up his phone and checked his email. Amid a bunch of sales emails, he saw one from Channel Twelve. He scrolled down and clicked it open.

> Hi Jasper!
>
> We are doing follow-ups with some of our Feel-Good Friday guests for Valentine's Day. The team checked Hop's Heaven socials, and it looks like you two are still going strong. Would you and Zaina like to be part of the Valentine's Day feature? It will be part of the eight-a.m. hour on this Friday's Feel Good. We can do the whole thing via Zoom.

Jasper stared at the email. Should he say thanks, but no thanks? Even though Zaina had withheld information from him, he wouldn't decide for her. Tomorrow morning, he'd call her and see if she wanted to do this and fulfill their deal or if she was as done as he was. He wasn't even sure if he could fake being part of a happy couple at this point. Taking an ax to the futon had helped, but he was still upset with Zaina and would be until he had a rational explanation from her own mouth explaining why she'd done what she did. He knew his anger would continue to simmer in the background. There was no way he could fake it with her. He wasn't the actor she was.

The only reason he'd been able to look so consumed by her in their videos was because he was. It had always been her, ever since she'd been his first kiss. He clicked out of his email box and went on his camera app. He scrolled through looking for the uncut video from the night they'd had dinner at Hop's Heaven and shared that kiss.

Jasper played the video with the sound off watching Zaina's face. The way her eyes were trained on his lips when he spoke, how she'd caressed his forearm while he was telling her an anecdote that he didn't even remember tonight. She'd lean in toward him as he'd dipped his chin about to kiss her and she'd taking a tiny breath. That couldn't have been all acting, could it? Did she despise him that much? He watched the video on repeat, looking for clues. If only he knew what she'd been thinking. Maybe she had liked him, but maybe she wasn't ready to trust him yet? His eyes felt heavy and while things were still very unresolved, his fatigue finally pulled him into sleep.

***

ZAINA

Zaina woke up with a start, her alarm blaring. *How could it be nine-thirty already?* She was meeting the girls for brunch at Jesse's Pub at ten a.m. She jumped out of bed, leaving the bed unmade and went to her dresser to pull out some clothes. Sometimes she liked to dress up for their brunches, but today, she was late and not feeling it. She rummaged until she found a decent pair of black yoga pants and an old favorite black cable-knit sweater. This would do and look slightly better than showing up for brunch in sweats. She took a quick shower, moisturized, and threw on some foundation and eyeliner. It was only a few minutes after ten when she started her car. She sent a quick *I'm running late* text to the group chat and headed out.

Ten minutes later, she was parked and rushing across the parking lot at Jesse's. She pushed open the door and stood at the host stand, scanning the tables looking for Devin and Nicole. Zaina saw Nicole waving from a booth tucked away from most of the crowd. She walked over and sat down next to Devin.

"About time you got here, Z. Now we can order a pitcher of mimosas. My throat is parched," Devin said and waved down someone from the waitstaff.

"Sorry about that. Even though I did nothing last night, I overslept. The worst part is I feel like I didn't get any sleep. I was tossing and turning all night," Zaina said.

"Huh," said Nicole, "Anything going on with Jasper?"

Zaina waved her off. "I don't want to talk about him right now. Let's go hit the buffet."

"Fair enough. I hope they have eggs benedict today. Get a move on now, Zaina," Devin scooted toward Zaina, who got out of the booth. The three women filled their plates with food and were soon back at the table.

"How's everything going with Ethan, Devin?" Zaina asked, trying to keep the conversation away from Jasper and her.

"It's been amazing. What a difference! He is patient, and he has the energy to keep up with the twins. I haven't been this happy in a long time. The entire house is happier these days."

Zaina grabbed Devin's hand, "I'm so happy to hear that! You deserve less stress; you've been doing too much for too long."

"Thank you, hon. Now, how are things with you and Jasper? Do you have more fake dating to do, or are you two ready to admit your feeling are real?" Devin inquired.

Zaina's cheeks pinked, "W-well, actually, I think we are done."

"Oh, no!" said Nicole, "I watched your live tarot reading, and I thought things were going very well. You two were all moony over each other."

Zaina rolled her eyes, "He's not interested in me. He is going to franchise his business and make millions and that's all he cares about."

Nicole frowned. "I don't know why you think that. I mean, sure, he wants to have a successful business, but it's obvious he cares about you."

Zaina bit her lip. "I know it because I tested him, and he failed."

"What does that mean, Z?" Devin asked as she cut a piece of her eggs benedict and popped it in her mouth. "Lord, this is as good as I hoped." She sighed.

"Can I try a piece, Dev?"

"Nic, it's a buffet. Go get your own."

Nicole gave Devin puppy dog eyes, "Please?"

"Okay, fine," Devin put a piece of her eggs benedict on Nicole's plate.

"You're the best, Dev." She chewed the crunchy muffin, savory ham and creamy egg with sauce. "This is amazing. I need Sean to make me some at home."

Zaina jumped on the chance to change the topic, "Is Sean living at your place now, Nic?"

Nicole adjusted her collar. "No, he isn't living with me. He basically spends every night there, however."

Zaina reached over and squeezed her friend's hand. "I'm so happy for you. I'm sure when you are ready, he'll be happy to live with you. Heck, I think he is going to propose sometime soon."

Nicole looked off into the distance where she could see Sean at the omelet station. "I'm in no hurry for a ring. I know he's the one and it will happen when it happens."

Devin, Nicole, and Zaina sighed.

"Now, back to you and Jasper. How did you test him?" Nicole asked, raising an eyebrow.

Zaina explained how she'd asked Mark to meet with Jasper and how she hadn't told Jasper that she'd made the meeting happen or that she was related to Mark. She talked about how she didn't want to be with someone who would say they would put their family first and then spend all their time focused instead on money and business success. She told them about how she'd finally found out the reason Jasper had ghosted her in high school was because his family didn't approve of her, because her family didn't have money.

Devin and Nicole did an unusually good job of just letting Zaina talk. When she finished, Nicole spoke. "Can I say something?"

"Sure, go ahead," Zaina said.

"It seems like, and I'm sure, this wasn't your end goal, but didn't you undermine any trust Jasper might have in you by tricking him?"

"I, ah, didn't think of that."

Devin chimed in, "I'm sorry, it's probably the type A in me, but I don't understand the issue. What's wrong with being successful?"

"It's not being successful per se. I just don't want to find myself married to someone who's always working. I want to be first and when we have a family, I want our family to be first."

Devin said, "You know that I'm the blunt one in our friendship, so I will not sugarcoat this. We, and by we, I mean everyone who knows you and Jasper and everyone on the Internet who's been watching your videos, can see that you two care about each other, and I know you know the chemistry is off the charts."

"The best night of my life was iced-in with Jasper," Zaina admitted.

"I think you need to ask yourself, why are you trying to sabotage this? Just because Jasper has a dream, doesn't meet that he would put it before you and your potential family. What if instead of trying to trick him, you'd talked to him about your feelings and your fears like grown people do?"

Tears stung Zaina's eyes; she felt awful. She took a shaky breath and tried to speak around the lump in her throat. "You're right, I went about it all wrong, and to be fair, my mom warned me."

"I've always liked your mom," interjected Nicole.

"I've got to decide if I'm going to trust Jasper or not."

"Yes, you do," said Devin.

Zaina's phone rang. She looked down at it. "Shit, it's Jasper."

"Go on, answer it!" said Nicole.

Zaina answered the phone, "Hello."

"Hi Zaina, you got a second?"

"Sure, what's up?" she could feel her pulse race. She wasn't ready to be confronted with what she'd done.

"I was going to tell you we could just forget about this fake dating thing," Jasper began.

Zaina gulped and continued listening.

"But then Channel Twelve reached out. They want to do a follow up with us for their Valentine's Day show on Friday. So, I didn't want to decide for you. I wanted to make sure I told you about what they'd asked. Unlike your recent behavior, I'm being upfront with you."

Zaina's face burned. "Um, thank you. I know it's more than I deserve. Do you want to do it?"

"Honestly, I don't know. I'll leave it up to you."

Zaina panicked. She didn't know what to do. "Can you hold on a minute?"

"I guess," he said flatly.

Zaina put her phone on mute. "Channel Twelve wants to do a follow up with us on their Friday show. Jasper wants to know if I want to do it or not. He says the decision is mine."

"What's your first instinct?" Nicole asked.

Zaina thought for a moment, "We should finish what we started."

"Then do it," Devin said and poured the last of the mimosa pitcher into their glasses.

Zaina took the phone off mute. "I thought about it, and I think we should finish what we started."

Jasper's voice rose, "You do? Then I'll tell them we are in."

"It's a plan. You'll let me know the details?"

"I'll text you."

Zaina hung up the phone. "We will be on the show Friday."

"This fake relationship has more twists and turns than any of the reality shows I've been watching lately," said Nicole.

"Try being in it!" Zaina said.

"Watching all this play out, I'm glad I'm a boring old married person. Best of luck to you, Zaina. I'm glad I'm done with the drama of dating." Devin said, and she clinked her glass against Zaina's.

"I think I'm ready to be over it as well." She raised her glass and took a long swallow of her drink.

"Don't forget, the group chat is always here for you. Maybe if you'd let us know what you were planning with Mark and Jasper, we could have talked you out of it," Nicole said.

Zaina stiffened. "I'm still not convinced it was a terrible idea. I did what I needed to do, but I will consider getting some feedback from you two before I scheme again. Maybe."

Devin just shook her head, and Nicole frowned.

Chapter Twenty-Five

❤

JASPER

On Thursday afternoon, Jasper got all the details from Channel Twelve for the Feel Good Friday and texted Zaina. He had hoped after they'd talked on Sunday, she would call or text him to apologize for misleading him, but that hadn't happened. The circumstances were different, but he couldn't help but think maybe he could now understand how she'd felt when he ignored her in high school. Jasper had spent this week grappling with his feelings for Zaina, and he had come to no conclusion. He wished he knew what was going on in her head.

"Hey Jasper, penny for your thoughts?" asked Kathy, who was sitting at the bar this afternoon enjoying the new Hop's Heaven non-alcoholic beverage, All Taste No Hangover.

Jasper startled, "Sorry, I was daydreaming there."

"You look sad. Anything you want to talk about?"

Jasper paused and then slowly nodded. "Yes, I would like to talk about it. I could really use your perspective."

"I'm all ears," Kathy said. She closed her laptop and gave Jasper her full attention.

"It's this thing with me and Zaina."

"Is there trouble in paradise? I thought things were going well."

"Truth be told, Kathy. It's all been a sham."

"What are you saying, Jasper?"

"You're probably going to think this is crazy, but Zaina and I made an agreement to fake date."

"Are you serious? I write fake dating and fake engagements all the time! It's very popular in romance novels. However, I can't say I've ever met anyone who actually did it in real life."

"Now you have."

"This makes so much more sense now. I thought it was strange the way you two were acting," Kathy continued, more to herself than him, "I should have known." Then she asked, "Is the fake dating the problem? How long are you going to keep it up?"

"Everything was fine at first. We were having fun and before I knew it, I couldn't stop thinking about her. I think I fell in love with Zaina the night of the ice storm, and I know, I know she felt something for me. Maybe it wasn't love, but she cared about me. Now I don't know what to think."

"What changed?"

"I've been going over every date, every text, I've been watching the videos we made, wracking my brain trying to answer that question."

"And did you come up with anything?"

"I think something I said or did around that tarot reading scared her and it just got worse from there." Jasper ran a hand through his shoulder length dark hair. A couple of plumbers at the end of the bar gave the 'another round' hand symbol. "I'll be right back Kathy." He poured a couple of pints and walked them over to the plumbers and returned to his conversation with Kathy.

Kathy sipped her drink and listened to Jasper continue the story. "You know how I've been working really hard to find investors so I can franchise the Hop's Heaven concept?"

Kathy gestured around the taproom, "Everyone who comes here knows that."

"Yeah, well, so I thought that because of our fake dating—which Zaina called our viral marketing scheme — that I had connected with Mark Anderson of ADM Investments."

"Oh no, Jasper, did you get catfished?"

"I almost wish I had. Zaina set up the meeting."

Kathy frowned. "How was that a bad thing?"

Jasper tapped the bar with each word for emphasis. "She. Didn't. Tell. Me. She. Set. It. Up."

Kathy cocked her head. "Why would she do that?"

"And the icing on the cake, or as I like to say, the foamy head on the beer—"

Kathy laughed once loudly.

Jasper continued, "Turns out, Mark Anderson is Zaina's stepdad."

"Wow."

"Yeah, wow! I didn't know until Mark told me himself. He came into the meeting thinking I knew Zaina had set up the meeting and that he was her stepfather. I felt like a complete idiot."

"Of course! You must have felt betrayed. Did Zaina say why she didn't tell you?"

"No, we've barely talked since. I don't even know if I would have called Zaina, but Channel Twelve wants to do a follow-up with us."

"Are you going to do the follow up?"

"Yes, we are, but I'm so confused, Kathy. Why did Zaina trick me? And why does she want to do the follow up tomorrow?"

Kathy held up her empty glass. "This calls for a refill. I love the new non-alcoholic beer. I can't tell the difference; it tastes just like the real thing to me."

"Thanks for the review. I'm glad you approve! I've been working for a long time on a non-alcoholic beer that has all the flavor of our real beers." He poured her a glass and one for himself.

Kathy lifted her glass and Jasper followed suit. "Cheers," she said, and they clinked their glasses and took a drink. Then she spoke. "Based on what I know of you and Zaina, and my decades of writing about love, I can offer some opinions and advice." She reached over and patted Jasper's hand, "And Jasper, please don't think you have to take my advice. I won't take it personally if you don't."

"I'm desperate here, Kathy. Please give me all your opinions and advice. Let me just go check on the end of the bar and then I'm all ears."

Jasper was back in a flash. "Give it to me straight, Kath."

"We can eliminate her not caring about you. If she didn't, she wouldn't have gone to the trouble of setting up that meeting and not telling you. I know it sounds ass backwards, but it's true. Also, I can't imagine she'd want to do the follow up tomorrow if she had stopped caring. Why else would she agree to going on TV and pretending you two are still dating?"

"If that's true, and I hope it is, why didn't she tell me she set up the meeting and why didn't she tell me who her stepdad was?"

"I can only guess—"

"Of course, I appreciate you giving me any ideas to make sense out of this."

"Maybe she thought if you knew who her stepdad was that she couldn't be sure you really liked her and not that you were using her to get to her stepfather. My guess is something like that might be a concern for her, since you talk about your business dream and finding investors pretty often."

"Got it, so you are saying I'm annoying, yammering on about my big goals to everyone I know. This is so embarrassing."

"Jasper, don't beat yourself up. You like to talk about your goals, and you also listen to anyone who wants to talk your ear off about anything. If you were truly annoying, you wouldn't have such a devoted clientele. Your beer is delicious, but you are the one that makes this place a community."

Jasper felt a lump in his throat. He took a sip of his beer and tried to clear his throat, but his words still came out a little hoarse. "That means the world to me. Thank you so much."

Kathy patted his hand again, "Now when it comes to why she set up the meeting in the first place and why she didn't tell you, that I'm not sure about. However, it reminds me of a book I wrote years ago. My main character was afraid to trust the man she was falling in love with, so she set him up to see if he would choose business over her. I can't believe I am sitting here in the middle of a life imitating art situation. This is the kind of thing you read in a book or watch on TV, but here we are! Do you think that could be it? Is she having trouble trusting you enough to let herself love you?"

"Honestly, Kathy, that would almost be a dream scenario. I'm sure there is a way I can show her she can trust me." The frown was off his face now and the little furrow between his brows smoothed.

"I'm so happy I could help! A couple more pieces of advice, be sure you love this girl before you go any further. I don't think she deserves another heartbreak and if you decide you are all in for Zaina, you're going to need to show her in a big way."

"Gotcha, show her in a big way. Make her feel safe to be with me."

"Exactly."

"How can I ever repay you, Kathy?"

Kathy put her finger to her lips. "Give me the rights to your story so I can sell it to a streaming service?"

Jasper laughed a belly laugh. "Not a chance, lady!"

Kathy joined him in laughing.

Chapter Twenty-Six

♥

ZAINA

Feel Good Friday morning dawned early for Zaina, who was up at six a.m. trying to decide what to wear. She didn't know how much of her would be on camera since they were doing their segment via Zoom. She finally decided on a solid black turtleneck and long silver filigree earrings. Zaina looked in the mirror and saw her dark brown roots peeking out from her scalp. She should have made the time to get her hair color touched up earlier in the week. *Too Late Now.*

Butterflies fluttered in her stomach, she felt too unsettled to eat and she wasn't sure if the anxiety was because she'd be on live TV or if it was because she'd be in the same room as Jasper for the first time since he'd realized her deception. With each passing moment, she doubted her decision to test Jasper more and more.

She was almost ready to admit she should have listened to her mom and had a conversation with Jasper about her worries instead of tricking him. Zaina sighed and rubbed her temples. To add insult to injury, she'd continued to stew all week, too stuck in her own fears to contact Jasper. Now it was too late. She'd be seeing him in half an hour and the likelihood she was going to walk in and puke on his shoes was more certain by the minute.

Zaina checked the time. She'd agreed to meet Jasper at Hop's Heaven by seven a.m. so that they could go over what they were going to say and make sure all technical glitches could be avoided. Plus, Jasper liked to make sure they looked as photogenic as possible when the camera was on, especially since this time they'd be using Jasper's work computer.

Zaina frowned. She didn't know how she was going to survive practically sitting in Jasper's lap, in the room where they'd had amazing sex, doing a live segment that people from Indiana to Wisconsin were going to watch while eating their breakfast cereal. She locked her front door and trudged downstairs; she wished this was over with already, but she couldn't force herself to move faster. She opened her car door and got in, shivering as she waited for the car to warm up. She hunched over as she drove to Hop's Heaven. Jasper's car was in the parking lot. Her mouth was dry, and her tongue felt thick as she tried to lick her lips. Could she be having an allergic reaction to conflict?

She opened the door and walked into the brewery. Zaina took off her gloves and rubbed her sweaty hands on her jeans. She walked with a heavier step and rattled her keys; she didn't want to come up on Jasper unawares. She heard someone stirring from the direction of his office. This was it. Her breathing was shallow, and she couldn't look him in the eyes.

"Hey there," he said in a soft voice.

Zaina forced herself to move her eyes from his chest. He was wearing a burnt orange henley that was perfectly fitted to accent his lean waist and broad shoulders. Her eyes moved up, and she saw his adam's apple bob and then her eyes were on his plump lips. She licked her own. Zaina willed herself to look up into his eyes, but she found she was frozen on his mouth, unable to look up or to speak.

"Thanks for coming early so we can go over what we are going to do this morning." Jasper said, and she noticed a rasp in his throat that surprised her. It broke the hold she had on herself.

"Are you okay? You sound like you have a cold."

Jasper cleared his throat. "I'm just run down, lack of sleep. I'll be fine."

Without thinking, Zaina moved closer and put the back of her hand on his forehead. "You feel warm," she said. She slid her hand down until she was cupping his jaw. He put a hand on her waist. Her chest tightened. She'd missed being close to him.

"Jasper," she started.

"Yes, Zaina?" The way he said her name with that extra roughness in his voice made her shiver. He rubbed her arms. "Are you cold? Sorry, it gets chilly here in the morning. Let's go to my office. I have a heater going in there."

"It's not that. I mean, I'm not cold." Zaina took a deep breath and steeled herself. She balled her hands into fists at her side. "I need to say something before we go any further. I should have this before now, but I was just stuck. I couldn't make myself do it."

Jasper put his hands in his pockets.

"Okay, here's the thing. I've been mad at you for so long and then we started fake dating and I got so confused. I want to be with you, but I don't know if I can trust you. That's why I tested you."

Jasper blurted out, "Why don't you trust me? Are you still holding on to what I did when I was a dumb kid?"

"No, well, honestly, I held on to that, until recently. Now I don't trust that you'd put me, you'd put us, above making money."

Jasper ran a hand through his hair. The muscle in his jaw ticked as he clenched his teeth. "And that's why you set up a meeting and didn't tell me Mark was your stepfather."

"I had to know what you would do!" she explained.

"What exactly was I supposed to do?"

"Once you found out he was my stepfather, you'd tell him you wouldn't want to mix business and family."

Jasper shook his head. "What happened was I looked like a babbling idiot. The meeting went nowhere, and I said I was concerned it was a conflict of interest!"

Zaina felt her face flush. "I realize now it was a stupid thing for me to do. I'm sorry! I should have just told you my fears."

"Yes, you should have." His phone alarm went off. "Crap, the segment is in twenty minutes. If you still want to do it?"

Zaina nodded, "Yes, unless you..."

"Let's finish what we started," he said.

Zaina followed him into his office. "You got rid of the futon?"

Jasper gave a half smile. "Yep, it needed to go." He sat down behind his desk. "Pull over a chair and come sit by me so we can see how we look on camera."

Zaina pulled over a wooden desk chair and when it was about six inches away from Jasper, she sat down. This would be close enough, she hoped. Jasper turned on the camera, but Zaina wasn't in the shot. Jasper turned in his chair, gripped the arm of her chair, and pulled her next to him.

"That's better. Now we are both in the frame. We only have a few minutes before we need to be in the Zoom green room. Do you trust me enough to let me speak first?" he asked.

She couldn't tell if his voice sounded harsh because he was coming down with a cold or if he was angry with her. She put her hand on his arm. "Jasper, if I could take it back, I would. I'm so sorry."

He turned and looked in her eyes, searching. "Do you trust me now?"

"I-I," her heart dropped, "I do trust you, as much as a can."

"Zaina," he whispered, and the Zoom connected.

"Zaina, Jasper, thanks for doing this segment today. We are going to go to you after the weather, so just sit tight here in this green room and when it's time, you'll hear the weather report and then I'll move you two into the station's Zoom," said the producer.

"Got it," said Jasper and Zaina in unison.

Jasper reached over and took Zaina's hand. His hand was sweaty, but she held on tight. It wasn't like him to be nervous. She looked at his profile. His dark hair fell in soft waves to his shoulders, his face was smooth and stubble free. His pulse was beating on his neck and she wanted to reach over and wrap him in a hug. She wanted to be enveloped in that palo santo scent of his.

"Tell us some good news about the Valentine's Day weekend weather, Suzy Snow!" John Johnson said.

"Warm weather is moving in, and we'll enjoy a weekend with above normal temperatures and no precipitation! So, get out there and make some memories with your sweetheart!"

"That's wonderful news, Suzy! Any chance we are done with snow for this winter?" Chrissy White asked.

Suzy put her hand on her stomach and laughed. "No chance! We have a cold front moving in next week that almost guarantees a snow day!" Suzy said.

"Winter weather, isn't it wild!? And speaking of wild, next we are checking in with everyone's favorite craft brewer, Jasper Kane, and the runner who fell for him, Zaina Evans," John Johnson said.

"Thanks for joining us this morning," Chrissy Snow said. "What do you two have planned for Valentine's Day?"

Jasper smiled and began speaking. "Thanks for inviting us back on Feel Good Friday. Zaina doesn't know what I'm about to say."

"Oooo," said Suzy Snow.

Zaina chewed on her bottom lip, very uncertain of where this was going. Sweat broke out and the back of her shirt was now clinging to her.

Jasper continued speaking. "After the video of the race went viral. I asked Zaina if she would help me with a viral marketing campaign. I told her all we needed to do was to pretend to be dating and post videos to raise my social media profile."

Tears stung Zaina's eyes and her nose got stuffy as Jasper talked.

"I did all of this because I wanted to find investors for my business. My goal for so long has been to franchise Hop's Heaven, and I was willing to deceive everyone to make that happen. I'm sorry for tricking all of you."

Then he turned to Zaina. Zaina's chest warmed as the butterflies swirled in her stomach.

"Zaina, I love you. I'm telling the world about our fake dating because I want you to know how much you mean to me. Business is a means to an end. You are my heart."

Zaina smiled widely as the tears ran down her face. Her mouth was dry as dust. She licked her lips and spoke. "Jasper, you know you are the last person I ever thought I could fall for," she sniffed. Jasper leaned over and wiped a tear from her cheek. "And then you show me how much I can trust you. Jasper Kane, I love you more than I ever thought possible." She felt like her heart would burst if she didn't kiss him right now. She put her hands on his cheeks, leaned in and kissed him with her whole heart.

The new crew started clapping and cheering. The video showed a split screen of Jasper and Zaina kissing side by side, with the news crew behind the anchor desk.

"The dating might have started out fake, but I know a proper kiss when I see it," Jake Boreman winked.

Suzy Snow clapped her hands. "I think they were the only two people watching those videos who didn't realize they were in love!"

"Jasper, Zaina," Chrissy White paused. Zaina regretfully pulled herself aways from Jasper and they turned back to the screen.

"We're here," said Jasper.

"Friends, I think I can speak for all of Channel Twelve and many of the people in our audience who appreciate you two coming clean." The rest of the anchor desk nodded.

"Thanks again for joining us today! Now we need to find out if there are any delays on the roadways," John Johnson said.

The screen blinked, and the Zoom ended. The camera turned off, and Zaina turned to Jasper.

"I can't believe you did that! What if you don't get a franchise deal now?" Zaina said.

"Zaina, I don't care. I realized after the meeting with Mark, I don't need a Hop's Heaven in every state in the USA. Success comes in many forms. My brewery here is thriving and my beers win medals. What I do need is you."

Zaina's insides were melting. "Jasper, let's get out of here."

"You sure?"

Zaina nodded, "I want to show you how much I appreciate what you did. No one has ever put me first. You put your business on the line for me!"

Jasper stood and pulled Zaina up. He bent down and kissed her. His tongue slid into her mouth, and she entwined her tongue in his. She wrapped her arms around his neck, needing to be closer to him. Then he pulled back, gasping for air. His hands were on her waist, and she was tempted to move them to her ass. She needed him now. "Let's go," she said breathlessly.

"Where do you want to go, Z?"

"Your house? My house? Wherever there is a bed?"

"Do we need a bed?" he whispered in her ear.

"I'm about thirty seconds away from saying the desk will work."

Jasper walked over and took his coat off the coat rack. "Get your coat. We're going to my place. I don't have to be back here until four today."

"Hannah is working at the shop today. I'll text her I'll be there at four."

"Fantastic," Jasper said, giving her his signature smile.

She put on her coat, then they held hands and ran out to the car.

Chapter
Twenty-Seven

♥

JASPER

Jasper's erection had pushed his jeans to their breaking point. He glanced to his side, admiring Zaina's profile as she texted her employee. Her neck was bare, and he marked with his eyes the line he would kiss going from just under her ear, down her neck. He couldn't wait to kiss the hollow between her collarbones.

A car honked behind them. Jasper looked up at the green light and hit the gas. Only two more turns and he'd be home. A couple of minutes later, he pulled into his driveway. The garage door opened, and he pulled in, not even bothering to click the door closed. He put the car in park.

They both unlatched their seatbelts and rushed out of the car. Jasper threw open the door and Zaina followed him into the house. Zaina started unlacing her boots and Jasper toed off his shoes and socks. Need consumed him; he had to get his hands on her. He couldn't wait a minute longer. The second she stood with her shoes off, he picked her up. She wrapped her legs around his narrow waist. She pushed the hair off his face and kissed him, her tongue entering his mouth. As they kissed, Zaina rubbed against him, and he could feel her hardened nipples through her shirt. *My God, is she not wearing a bra?* He couldn't wait to find out.

He strode down the hall and upstairs to his room. He kicked the door open and dropped Zaina on his bed. Jasper looked into her eyes. Her pupils were wide with desire, crowding out the rich brown of her irises. He reached behind him, grabbing the fabric of his shirt, and pulled it off. She bit her bottom lip, and he felt warmth pool low in his belly as her eyes moved from his chest down to his abs as he unbuttoned his pants. He moaned as she reached down and unzipped his jeans. He was hard as granite. He shucked off his jeans, letting them take his underwear with them. Jasper stood before her and began stroking himself.

"I need you inside me," she said. She pulled her turtleneck off, and he leaned across the bed and took one of her pebbled nipples in his mouth, rolling it with his tongue. She moaned quietly as he laved her nipple, her hand reaching down to grasp his cock. Her small hand was barely large enough to fully wrap around him.

She stroked him as he switched breasts. He sucked a small mark just about her right nipple, then he pushed her back onto the bed. He pulled off her pants, leaving her lacy panties on. Jasper needed to taste her now. It had been too long since he'd had her juices in his mouth.

Jasper slowly kissed her panty line, moving from her flat stomach down to the delicate flesh of her inner thigh. He bunched the lace of her underwear, rubbing the rough fabric against her clit as his mouth made its way toward her folds. Jasper sighed with contentment when the vanilla scent of her was in his mouth and in his nose. He could live here between her legs. He pulled off her panties and tossed them on the floor and then he went back to lavishing attention on her core. He flicked her swollen nub with his tongue, moving faster now, and Zaina bucked against him.

Her hands were in his hair, directing him, and he could tell she was close. He plunged two fingers into her wet pussy, and his balls tightened as he felt her muscles clench around his fingers. He moved in and out as his tongue swirled around her clit. She ground against him as she came. He stayed with her, giving light touches now as she came down, then Jasper looked up at her from between her thighs, slowly licking her off his fingers.

"Now it's your turn," she said, and he shivered. She scrambled up the bed away from him and patted the spot next to her.

"Yes ma'am," he said. He moved to her, and she straddled him, facing away so he had a glorious view of her pussy as she took him into her mouth. She licked her way down his throbbing cock. Tracing his veins with her tongue, she moved her mouth up to the top where she licked pre-cum off his tip and then she pushed down, sucking him in and out. Her head bobbed as she worked.

"You are so fucking good at blowing me, Z. I love having your pretty lips around my big cock."

He felt her chuckle against him, and it almost pushed him over the edge. "Love, let me fuck you now. I need your pussy around my cock," he begged.

She gave his balls one last squeeze and moved to his side. He leaned over and opened the nightstand drawer. He pulled out a condom and quickly put it on. To his surprise, she straddled him again. She leaned down and kissed him, then she wrapped her hands around his rock-hard cock and guided it into her opening. She slowly slid down until she was full of him. She began moving back and forth and he gripped her taut bottom, guiding them both in a rhythm. He'd planned to go slowly, but she wasn't having it as she rocked back and forth, faster and faster, and he let her sweep him away.

Zaina cried out, "Yes Jasper, just like that, yes!" and he couldn't hold back any longer. He spilled his seed as he listened to her moaning. They stayed together, enjoying the aftershocks, and later she slowly got off him. He quickly went to the bathroom to take care of the condom. When he came back to bed, she took a turn to use the bathroom.

They finally got to snuggle together in bed. He rubbed her back. "I'm so happy, Zaina," he said.

She played with a lock of his hair. "Me too," she said. "I still can't believe you did that this morning."

He kissed her nose. "I realized I could talk until I lost my voice, but you still wouldn't be able to fully trust me. I had to show you that you can trust me to put you first."

"Boy, did you," she kissed him. "I love you Jasper, and I have to tell you something. I want to make sure you know everything I need."

Jasper's large hand skimmed her body as he moved down her side and over to her breast. He cupped it. "Tell me so I can give it to you."

She took a deep, shuddering breath. "The reason I agreed to our fake dating is I wanted to use the money to start artificial insemination."

Jasper paused. "Your dream is to have a baby?"

Zaina rested her suddenly clammy hand on his hip. "That's my dream."

"Any reason specific reason you are going about it that way?"

"I only have the eggs. I need the sperm."

"So, you don't have to do artificial insemination? You could have a baby the old-fashioned way?"

"As far as I know," she was shivering now. Jasper pulled her to him and kissed the crown of her head.

"Zaina, I'm so glad you told me this. It may seem too soon, but please hear me out. I'm crazy in love with you. Thinking about having a baby with you makes my chest tighten in the best way."

Zaina pulled back and looked at him. Her eyes were shining. "Are you sure, Jasper?"

"I'm sure, Zaina, this feels so right. Remember when you read my cards? I get it now! The hanged man was me at a crossroads. I could choose to focus only on my business, and I'd be successful or I could stop ignoring what was calling to me—that's what the temperance card said, right?"

"Yes, that's a good way of looking at the reversed temperance card," Zaina said.

"I was ignoring love and family. What I learned from my parents wasn't a zeal for making money. What I learned from them, but tried to push away for many years, was how pointless money was without love and companionship. I want you. I want you to build a family with me. Let's have a baby, Zaina."

Zaina wrapped her arms around Jasper, burying her head in Jasper's chest. She began shaking.

"What's wrong, my love?" he said quietly.

"I never thought I could be this happy."

He kissed the tears off her cheeks.

"Should we start trying now?"

Zaina swatted his chest. "First you'll need to fill out an application, and we'll need to conduct a daddy interview."

"I'll take any test you want to give me."

Epilogue

❤

JASPER

Jasper double checked his pant's pocket. Every day for the past week, he'd gotten dressed and put the small black velvet box in his pocket. Every morning, he told himself this was the day he'd ask Zaina to marry him. She'd said she didn't need a husband, that he'd already given her everything she wanted and more, but he wanted to tie the knot. He wanted that silly piece of paper and all the government recognition, he even wanted the pomp and circumstance of going down the aisle. Heck, if it was what Zaina wanted he'd be happy if their ceremony meant dancing naked around the full moon. Whatever ceremony she wanted, she was getting. He put on his tie and checked the time on his phone.

"Zaina my love, the dinner is starting in twenty minutes. Are you almost ready to go?" He walked into the large closet where Zaina was standing in her bra and underwear. He licked his lips as he stared at her round bottom peeking out of her black panties. Her curves had grown lusher over the last couple of months, and he couldn't keep his hands off her. Jasper wrapped his arms around her waist, cradling the growing swell of her belly.

Zaina leaned back against him and whined, "I can't find anything that fits."

Jasper rubbed her stomach. "I'm sure you have something you can wear. You're not that huge, Z."

She lightly swatted his hand. "Rude! It's not my stomach that's the issue. It's these," she said, and she put his hands on her breasts. "I'm only five months pregnant and my boobs are already huge!" Jasper couldn't help himself; he unsnapped the front of her bra and began caressing Zaina's breasts. She moaned as he squeezed her pebbled nipples with his fingers. He kissed the nape of her neck, and he knew she could feel what she did to him. She pressed back into him a little harder and then he froze for a second, worried she was going to rub up against the ring box.

"Zaina, if we don't stop, we are going to miss the rehearsal dinner and Sean and Nicole will kill us, leaving our baby an orphan."

Zaina took his hand off her breast and slid it into her underwear. He moved his finger through her folds, feeling her slick wetness and the nub of her clit. He rubbed it despite his desire to get them to the dinner on time.

"Jasper, oh, that feels so good." She pressed against his hand. He braced himself as she rocked against him. "I can't get enough of you lately," she gasped. He took his free hand and cupped her breast, rubbing his thumb over her nipple. She shivered as he did. "My nipples are so sensitive, yes, just like that, so soft." He went back to focusing on her deliciously wet pussy. He stroked her, knowing exactly how she liked it, she gasped, and he knew she was about to come. "I-I t-hink that book is right, the second trimester is the horni-est! Yes, Jasper, yes! Right there!"

She bucked against his hand and he pulled her against him, his cock so hard he thought he might come in his pants. "Come for me, Zaina," he whispered in her ear, and he rubbed her bud furiously.

"Yes, baby, yes!" she screamed as she climaxed.

Jasper held Zaina as she came down from her high. He put his fingers in his mouth, sucking off her sweet juices. "My love, I think you taste even more delicious now." She turned around, facing him, her swollen belly between them. A lump formed in his throat. *This, right now, was perfect.* She put her arms around his neck and pulled him into her for a kiss.

He pulled back from her, and took the ends of her bra, and tried to clasp it. He squeezed a little harder to close the gap. Her basic bra had now become an overflowing push-up bra. He kissed the tops of each of her breasts. "I love you so much," he said, his voice cracking.

Jasper got down on one knee and pulled the black box out of his pocket. Zaina looked down at him and gasped. She put her hands over her mouth.

"Zaina, when I wake up in the morning and roll over, I see your beautiful face with your mouth open slightly and I hear a delicate snore and I know how comfortable you are around me."

Zaina smacked him on the chest.

"Ouch," he said exaggeratedly. "I look at you and I know you are my home. You are my family and I'm the luckiest man in the world. Like the King of Pentacles says, I have an abundance of riches.

His hands were shaking now, and he struggled to open the box. He finally popped it open. Inside the box was a platinum trinity knot ring. Zaina gasped, and he cleared his throat.

"Zaina, my love, will you marry me?"

She threw herself at him, knocking him down onto the floor of the closet.

"Yes, a million times, yes!"

He leaned up on his elbows, and Zaina took his face in her hands, kissing him. Jasper kissed her back. "Z," he said mid kiss.

"Mm?" Zaina said.

Jasper pulled himself up, keeping Zaina on his lap. He took her left hand in his, raised an eyebrow, and looked at Zaina's face. Her eyes were shining with tears. "Can I put the ring on your finger?"

"Jasper, how did you know? This ring, it's perfect!"

Jasper expanded his chest in pride, "I've been listening and paying attention when you are working on your witchy stuff, and if you want to have a Wiccan or a pagan ceremony or if you want to go full on bridezilla and have five hundred guests, I'm all in."

Tears were streaming down Zaina's face, taking her makeup with it. Jasper put the ring on her finger and then he leaned over and pulled a T-shirt off its hanger and used that to wipe the tears off Zaina's face. "You look more beautiful every day," he said, cupping her face.

She leaned over and kissed him. "I'm getting bigger every day. Maybe we'll wait and bring our baby to the wedding." Jasper rubbed her belly, and then his phone alarm went off.

"We are going to be so late!" Zaina said, jumping off Jasper. "And I still haven't figured out what to wear!"

Jasper looked around the closet. "You could wear pajamas if you wanted to. No one is going to be paying attention to you. Tonight is all about Nicole and Sean."

Zaina nodded. "You know, you're right. I'm over thinking this." She flipped back through her closet and found a flowy empire-waisted dress.

Jasper sat on the floor of the closet and watched Zaina don the dress. The square cut of the neckline only enhanced Zaina's overflowing cleavage. His pants tightened, and he had to adjust himself. "Fair warning, I'm not going to be able to keep my eyes or my hands off you in that dress."

Zaina's cheeks were pink. "I'll throw on some new makeup and we'll be ready to go."

***

ZAINA

Zaina couldn't stop looking at her hand clasped in Japer's. She was engaged! Was it cool to run into Jesse's Pub and tell Devin and Nicole, or was it bad form to announce her engagement at her best friend's rehearsal dinner? Who was she kidding? Devin and Nicole were going to jump up and down with joy for her. Oh my gosh, she needed to call her mom. She was still wrapping her head around becoming a grandma, and now she was going to be someone's mother-in-law!

Jasper parked the car. Zaina started to get out of the car, but he put a hand on her knee. "You stay there. I'll get the door for my fiancé."

She rolled her eyes. "Jasper, you don't need to do that."

He was already out of the car. "I know, but I want to!" He ran around the car and opened her door. He held out his hand. "Future Mrs. Kane and Baby Kane."

Zaina pushed herself out of her seat. Being short and short-waisted, she knew she was going to have a heck of a time getting out of cars, couches, and beds as their baby continued to grow. She stood up and adjusted her dress.

"Would you like me to help you fix the girls?

"Since when do we call my boobs 'the girls'?"

Jasper just waggled his eyebrows as she finished fixing her dress, then he held out his large hand, and she took it.

"I'm never going to tire of holding hands with you," she said hoarsely.

"Do you need a tissue? Did you remember to put on the waterproof mascara?" Jasper asked with concern.

Zaina dabbed her eyes with her fingers. "Today, I truly don't know if it's the hormones, or that I'm deliriously happy."

They looked at each other.

"Both?" they said in unison and laughed as they walked into Jesse's Pub.

Sean and Nicole were standing at the host stand.

Zaina looked at Sean, "Boy, do you clean up well! I don't think I've ever seen you in a suit." Sean chuckled and gave Zaina a hug. "I tried to avoid them at all costs."

Jasper gave Nicole a hug as well. "Nicole, you look beautiful. You are glowing."

She kissed his cheek, "Thank you, Jasper. "

Zaina couldn't contain herself any longer, "Nicole, Sean, I know this is probably super tacky, but..." then she held up her arm so her engagement ring faced them.

"O.M.G.!" Nicole squealed. "You guys! This is the best news ever! It's not tacky at all! I mean it would be if y'all had done this tomorrow on the wedding day, or during the rehearsal dinner, but since you didn't, I'm good."

Zaina and Nicole hugged, rocking back and forth, and Jasper and Sean fist bumped.

"Who would have thought?" asked Sean.

Jasper nodded. "This year has been better than anything I could have dreamed."

"Is Devin here yet?" Zaina asked.

"The Belmont clan is right behind you," Devin said.

Devin and Ben walked in, holding hands. Behind them Ethan was corralling Franklin and Liam who were wearing matching outfits.

Nicole grabbed Devin's hand, "Guess who just got engaged!?"

Devin eyes zeroed in on Zaina's left hand. "Z, I love the ring. Congratulations! Group hug!"

Devin, Zaina, and Nicole wrapped their arms around each other.

Ben shook Jasper's hand. "Congrats, my man. Looks like we'll be seeing a lot of each other from here on out."

Zaina looked over at Ethan, who was sitting down at a table with Franklin and Liam. It was hard to believe those were the same twins that had crawled under a grate and into his brewhouse last fall. "Say Devin, do you think maybe we can borrow Ethan when the baby is born?"

Devin stopped hugging Zaina. "Z, get your own manny!"

"Alright, alright. It was worth a try." Zaina shrugged. "Oh look, Mable joined the boys at the table."

Sean nodded. "Mable just got back from her summer abroad. I'm glad she could make the rehearsal dinner. Technically, we are cousins by marriage, but she's become a little sister to me."

Zaina squinted at Ethan and Mable's interaction. Ethan was speaking animatedly, and as Mable was laughing, she put a hand on his arm. Jasper sidled up to Zaina and wrapped an arm around her shoulder. "Look how cute they are," Zaina said. "It makes me want to give Mable a tarot reading."

"You should see if Ethan wants his cards read. Look what it did for me!"

Zaina stood on her tiptoes and kissed the tip of Jasper's nose. "Sometimes, I think we were inevitable. We just didn't know it."

Also By Victoria Hamel

♥

Book One in the Marley Creek Romance Series

No Gouda Without You

Get your copy of book one here: https://a.co/d/0avDaHZ

And Coming this Summer:

Book Three in the Marley Creek Romance Series

Is This Love Fur Real?

Preorder your copy here: https://a.co/d/8e7WOW3

Sign up for Victoria's free newsletter to stay up to date on her book news:

https://deft-crafter-9476.ck.page/profile

About the Author

♥

Victoria's love of writing began in grade school, where she won an award for a Mother's Day essay. She spent the better part of her childhood with her head in a book. In high school, she wrote love stories for her friends in which they'd meet their favorite bands or the movie star they had a crush on. Suffice it to say, Victoria was writing fan fiction before fan fiction was a thing. After spending many years starting and stopping writing in various genres, Victoria returned to her high school roots and decided to write romance.

Victoria Hamel lives in the Chicago area with her husband, three college-age kids and Bowie the dog. She has run three marathons and based on that experience, she feels qualified to say that reviewing her manuscript for errors was a more arduous task than literally running a marathon. She is a member of the Chicago North Romance Writers Group. When she isn't writing, Victoria volunteers for local democrat candidates, watches K-Dramas, or can be found blogging on her blog *First of All...*(https://victoria7401.blogspot.com)

No Gouda Without You is her debut novel and the first book in the Marley Creek Romance series. Book two, *Too Kölsch For*

Comfort is available April 30, 2024, you can order it via this link : *Too Kölsch For Comfort* https://a.co/d/0avDaHZ. Book three, *Is This Love Fur Real?* will be available this summer and you can preorder it via this link: https://a.co/d/8e7WOW3

Acknowledgements

♥

The Marley Creek Romance series would not exist if I hadn't started following Maria Sccoy's live videos on Facebook. Thanks to Maria and her writer-to-author program, I was able to make a plan to write not just one book, but a whole series of small town romance! If you've spent years wanting to write a book, check out All Write Well (www.allwritewell.com) it may be just what you need to finish that book!

Thanks so much to my husband Tom for his support. He is the best hype man! Even though he doesn't get romance books, he's still happy to be a sounding board and share my book news with everyone he meets.

Thanks to Kim Ehrenhaft for doing a beta read of *Too Kölsch For Comfort!* Huge thanks to Cheryl T for beta reading! I appreciate you!

Thank you to all the readers! I am so grateful for your time. There are so many books out there and you chose me!